Book 11

CIRQUE DU FREAK

THE SAGA OF DARREN SHAN

Lord of the Shadows

Book 11

CIRQUE DU FREAK

THE SAGA OF DARREN SHAN

Lord of the Shadows

by Darren Shan

LITTLE, BROWN AND COMPANY

New York Boston

Little, Brown and Company

Hachette Book Group USA
1271 Avenue of the Americas, New York, NY 10020
Visit our Web site at www.lb-teens.com

First U.S. Edition: May 2006

First published in Great Britain by Collins in 2004.

Library of Congress Cataloging-in-Publication Data

Shan, Darren
Lord of the shadows / by Darren Shan. — 1st U.S. ed.
p. cm. — (The saga of Darren Shan ; bk. 11)
Summary: When Darren Shan returns home, he is met by old enemies and scores to be settled, and with destiny certain to destroy him, the world seems doomed to fall to the Ruler of the Night.
ISBN 0-316-15628-0
[1. Vampires — Fiction. 2. Horror stories.] I. Title: At head of title: Cirque du Freak. II. Title.

PZ7.S52823Lore 2006
[Fic] — dc22 2005050420

10 9 8 7 6 5 4 3 2

Q-FF

Printed in the United States of America

Also in the CIRQUE DU FREAK series:

Cirque Du Freak (Book 1)
The Vampire's Assistant (Book 2)
Tunnels of Blood (Book 3)
Vampire Mountain (Book 4)
Trials of Death (Book 5)
The Vampire Prince (Book 6)
Hunters of the Dusk (Book 7)
Allies of the Night (Book 8)
Killers of the Dawn (Book 9)
The Lake of Souls (Book 10)

For:

Bas — my globetrotting pal

OBEs
(Order of the Bloody Entrails) to:
Maiko "Greenfingers" Enomoto
Megumi "The Voice" Hashimoto
"Queen" Tomoko Taguchi
"Eagle-eyed" Tomoko Aoki
Yamada "Papa" san
And everybody else on the Japanese Shan team who worked so hard to make June 2003 such a special time for me

Editing Crew:
Gillie "The Don" and Zoë "The Mom"

Guiding Lights:
The Christopher Little Posse

PROLOGUE

IN THE DISTANCE A WAVE of blood was building. Red, towering, topped with spitting heads of fire. On a vast plain, a mass of vampires waited. All three thousand or so faced the onrushing wave. At the rear, separated from the crowd, I stood alone. I was trying to push forward — I wanted to be with the rest of the clan when the wave hit — but an invisible force held me back.

As I struggled, roaring silently — my voice didn't work here — the wave swept ever nearer. The vampires pulled closer together, terrified but proud, facing their deaths with dignity. Some were pointing spears or swords at the wave, as though they could fight it back.

Closer now, almost upon them, half a mile high, stretching in an unbroken line across the horizon. A wave of crackling flames and boiling blood. The moon disappeared behind the crimson curtain and a blood-red darkness descended.

The foremost vampires were eaten by the wave. They screamed in agony as they were crushed, drowned, or burned to death, their bodies tossed about like pieces of cork within the heart of the scarlet wave. I reached out to them — my people! — and prayed to the gods of the vampires to free me, so that I could die with my blood-brothers and sisters. But still I couldn't break through the invisible boundary.

More vampires vanished beneath the breaking surf of fire and blood, lost to the wave of merciless red. A thousand lives extinguished . . . fifteen hundred warriors eliminated . . . two thousand souls sent soaring to Paradise . . . twenty-five hundred death howls . . . three thousand corpses, bobbing and burning in the flames.

And then only I was left. My voice returned, and with a desolate cry I collapsed to my knees and glared hatefully up at the crest of the wave as it teetered overhead. I saw faces within the walls of flaming blood — my friends and allies. The wave was taunting me with them.

Then I saw something hovering in the air above the wave, a creature of myth but oh so real. A dragon.

Long, glittering, scaled, terrifyingly beautiful. And on its back — a person. A figure of pulsating darkness. It was almost as though his body had been created from shadows.

The shadow man laughed when he saw me, and his laugh was a ghostly cackle, evil and mocking. At his command, the dragon swooped lower, so that it was only ten feet above me. From here I could see it's rider's features. His face was a mass of dancing patches of darkness, but when I squinted I recognized him — Steve Leopard.

"All must fall to the Lord of the Shadows," Steve said softly, and pointed behind me. "This is my world now."

Turning around, I saw a vast area of wasteland dotted with corpses. Over the dead bodies crawled giant toads, hissing black panthers, grotesque human mutants, and more nightmarish creatures and shapes. Cities burned in the far distance, and great mushroom clouds of smoke and flames filled the air overhead.

I faced Steve again and roared a challenge at him. "Face me on the ground, you monster! Fight me now!"

Steve only laughed, then waved an arm at the wave of fire. There was a moment of hushed calm. Then the wave crashed to earth around me and I was swept away, face burning, lungs filling with blood, surrounded by the bodies of the dead. But what terrified me most before I was swallowed by eternal blackness was that I'd snatched one final glimpse of the Lord of the Shadows before I died. And this time it wasn't Steve's face I saw — it was *mine.*

CHAPTER ONE

My eyes snapped open. I wanted to scream, but there was a hand over my mouth, rough and powerful. Fear gripped me. I lashed out at my attacker. Then my senses returned and I realized it was just Harkat, muffling my screams so that I didn't disturb any of the sleepers in the neighboring caravans and tents.

I relaxed and tapped Harkat's hand to show that I was OK. He released me and stepped back, his large green eyes alive with concern. He handed me a mug of water. I drank deeply from it, then wiped a shaking hand across my lips and smiled weakly. "Did I wake you?"

"I wasn't asleep," Harkat said. The grey-skinned Little Person didn't need much sleep and often went two or three nights without dozing. He took the mug from me and set it down. "It was a bad one this . . . time. You started screaming five or six . . . minutes ago, and only stopped now. The same nightmare?"

"Isn't it always?" I muttered. "The wasteworld, the wave of fire, the dragon, the . . . Steve," I finished quietly. I'd been haunted by the nightmare for almost two years, screaming myself awake at least a couple of times a week. In all those months I hadn't told Harkat about the Lord of the Shadows and that wretched face I always saw at the end of the nightmare. As far as Harkat knew, Steve was the only monster in my dreams — I didn't dare tell him that I was as scared of myself as I was of Steve Leopard.

I swung my legs out of my hammock and sat up. I could tell by the darkness that it was only three or four in the morning, but I knew I wouldn't be able to sleep anymore. The nightmare always left me shaken and wide awake.

Rubbing the back of my neck, I found myself studying Harkat out of the corner of my eye. Although he wasn't the source of my nightmares, I could trace their origins back to him. The Little Person had been built from the remains of a corpse. For most of his new life he hadn't known who he was. Two years ago, Mr. Tiny — a man of immense power, with the ability to travel through time — transported us to a barren wasteworld and sent us off on a quest to discover Harkat's previous identity. We fought a variety of wild creatures and twisted monstrosities before finally fishing Harkat's original body out of the Lake of Souls, a holding place for damned spirits.

Harkat used to be a vampire called Kurda Smahlt. He'd betrayed the vampire clan in a bid to prevent war with our blood-cousins, the purple-skinned vampaneze. To make up for his sins, he'd agreed to become Harkat Mulds and travel back into the past to be my guardian.

I'm Darren Shan, a Vampire Prince. I'm also one of the hunters of the Lord of the Vampaneze — a.k.a. Steve Leopard. Steve was destined to lead the vampaneze to victory over the vampires. If he won, he'd wipe us out entirely. But a few of us — the hunters — had the ability to stop him before he came fully into his powers. If we found and killed him before he matured, the war would be ours. By helping me as Harkat, Kurda hoped to help the clan and prevent their destined destruction at the hands of the vampaneze. In that way he could put right some of the wrongs he'd committed.

Having learned the truth about Harkat, we returned to our own world — rather, our own *time*. Because what we worked out later was that the wasteworld wasn't an alternative universe or Earth in the past, as we'd first thought — it was Earth in the future. Mr. Tiny had given us a glimpse of what was to come if the Lord of the Shadows came to power.

Harkat thought the ruined world would only come to pass if the vampaneze won the War of the Scars. But I knew about a prediction that I hadn't shared with anybody else. When the hunt for Steve was finally concluded, there would be one of two possible futures. In one, Steve became the Lord of the Shadows and destroyed the world. In the other future, the Lord of the Shadows was *me*.

That's why I woke in a cold sweat, to the sound of my own screams, so often. It wasn't just fear of the future, but fear of myself. Would I somehow play a part in creating the barren, twisted world I'd seen in the future? Was I damned to become a monster like Steve, and wreck all that I held dear? It seemed impossible, but the uncertainties gnawed away at me all the same, prompted by the ever-repeating nightmares.

I spent the time before dawn chatting with Harkat, small talk, nothing serious. He'd suffered terrible nightmares before finding out the truth about himself, so he knew exactly what I was going through. He knew what to say to calm me down.

When the sun rose and the Cirque camp started to come to life around us, we made an early start on our day's chores. We'd been with the Cirque Du Freak since returning from our grueling quest in the waste-world. We knew nothing about what was happening in the War of the Scars. Harkat wanted to return to Vampire Mountain, or at least make contact with the clan — now that he knew he had once been a vampire, he was more concerned than ever for them. But I held off. I didn't feel the time was right. I had a hunch that we were meant to remain with the Cirque, and that destiny would decide our course as and when it saw fit. Harkat strongly disagreed with me — we'd had some very heated arguments about it — but he reluctantly followed my lead, though I'd sensed recently that his patience was coming to an end.

We performed a variety of jobs around the camp, helping out wherever we were needed — moving equipment, mending costumes, feeding the Wolf Man. We were handymen. Mr. Tall — the owner of the Cirque Du Freak — had offered to find more responsible, permanent positions for us, but we didn't know when we'd have to leave. It was easier to stick to simple tasks and not get too involved in the long-term running of the show. That way we wouldn't be missed too much when the time came to part company with the freakish folk.

We'd been performing on the outskirts of a large

city, in an old, run-down factory. Sometimes we played in a big top that we transported around with us, but Mr. Tall always liked to take advantage of local venues whenever possible. This was our fourth and final show in the factory. We'd be moving on in the morning, to new pastures. None of us knew where we'd be going yet — Mr. Tall made those decisions and usually didn't tell us until we'd broken camp and were already on the move.

We put on a typically tight, exciting show that night, built around some of the longest-serving performers — Gertha Teeth, Rhamus Twobellies, Alexander Ribs, Truska the bearded lady, Hans Hands, Evra and Shancus Von. Usually the Vons rounded off the show, treating audiences to one final scare when their snakes slid from the shadows overhead. But Mr. Tall had been experimenting with different lineups recently.

Onstage, Jekkus Flang was juggling knives. Jekkus was one of the Cirque helpers, like Harkat and me, but tonight he'd been billed as a star attraction and was entertaining the crowd with a display of knife tricks. Jekkus was a good juggler, but his act was pretty dull compared to the others. After a few minutes, a man in the front row stood up as Jekkus balanced a long knife on the tip of his nose.

CHAPTER ONE

"This is rubbish!" the man shouted, climbing onto the stage. "This is meant to be a place of magic and wonder — not juggling tricks! I could see stuff like this at any circus."

Jekkus took the knife from his nose and snarled at the intruder. "Get off the stage, or I'll cut you up into tiny pieces!"

"You don't worry me," the man snorted, taking a couple of large paces over to Jekkus, so they were eye-ball to eyeball. "You're wasting our time and money. I want a refund."

"Insolent scum!" Jekkus roared, then lashed out with his knife and cut off the man's left arm just below the elbow! The man screamed and grabbed for the falling limb. As he was reaching for his lost forearm, Jekkus struck again and cut off the man's other arm in the same place!

People in the audience erupted with panic and surged to their feet. The man with the jagged stumps beneath his elbows tottered towards the edge of the stage, desperately waving his half arms around, face white with apparent shock. But then he stopped — and laughed.

The people in the front rows heard the laughter and stared up at the stage suspiciously. The man laughed again. This time his laughter carried farther, and people all around relaxed and faced the stage. As they watched, tiny hands grew out of the stumps of the man's arms. The hands continued to grow, followed by wrists and forearms. A minute later, the man's arms had returned to their natural length. He flexed his fingers, grinned, and took a bow.

"Ladies and gentlemen!" Mr. Tall boomed, appearing suddenly on stage. "Put your hands together for the fabulous, the amazing, the incredible *Cormac Limbs*!"

Everybody realized they'd been the victims of a practical joke — the man who'd stepped out of the audience was a performer. They clapped and cheered as Cormac sliced off his fingers one by one, each of which grew back quickly. He could cut off any part of his body — though he'd never tried chopping of his head! Then the show finished for real and the crowd poured out, babbling with excitement, wildly discussing the mystical mysteries of the sensational Cirque Du Freak.

Inside, Harkat and I helped with the cleaning up. Everyone involved was vastly experienced, and we could normally clear everything away within half an hour, sometimes less. Mr. Tall stood in the shadows while we worked. That was odd — he normally retired to his van after a show — but we took little notice of it. You grew used to oddness when you worked with the Cirque Du Freak!

As I was stacking several chairs, to be removed to a truck by other hands, Mr. Tall stepped forward. "A moment, please, Darren," he said, removing the tall red hat he wore whenever he went onstage. He took a map out of the hat — the map was much larger than the hat, but I didn't question how he'd fit it inside — and unrolled it. He held one end of the map in his large left hand and nodded for me to take the other end.

"This is where we are now," Mr. Tall said, pointing to a spot on the map. I studied it curiously, wondering why he was showing me. "And this is where we will be going next," he said, pointing to a town a hundred miles away.

I looked at the name of the town. My breath caught in my throat. For a moment I felt dizzy and a cloud seemed to pass in front of my eyes. Then my expression cleared. "I see," I said softly.

"You don't have to come with us," Mr. Tall said. "You can take a different route and meet up with us later, if you wish."

I started to think about it, then made a snap gut decision instead. "That's OK," I said. "I'll come. I want to. It . . . it'll be interesting."

"Very well," Mr. Tall said briskly, taking back

the map and rolling it up again. "We depart in the morning."

With that, Mr. Tall slipped away. I felt he didn't approve of my decision, but I couldn't say why, and I didn't give much thought to it. Instead I stood by the stacked-up chairs, lost in the past, thinking about all the people I'd known as a child, especially my parents and younger sister.

Harkat limped over eventually and waved a grey hand in front of my face, snapping me out of my daze. "What's wrong?" he asked, sensing my disquiet.

"Nothing," I said, with a confused shrug. "At least, I don't think so. It might even be a good thing. I . . ." Sighing, I stared at the ten little scars on my fingertips and muttered without looking up, "I'm going home."

CHAPTER TWO

ALEXANDER RIBS STOOD, rapped his rib cage with a spoon, and opened his mouth. A loud musical note sprang out and all conversation ceased. Facing the boy at the head of the table, Alexander sang, "He's green, he's lean, snot he's never seen, his name is Shancus — happy birthday!"

Everybody cheered. Thirty performers and helpers from the Cirque Du Freak were seated around a huge oval table, celebrating Shancus Von's eighth birthday. It was a chilly April day, and most people were wrapped up warmly. The table was overflowing with cakes, sweets, and drinks, and we were digging in happily.

When Alexander Ribs sat down, Truska — a woman who could grow her beard at will — stood and sung another birthday greeting. "The only things he fears is his mother's flying ears, his name is Shancus — happy birthday!"

Merla snapped one of her ears off when she heard that and flicked it at her son. He ducked and it flew high over his head, then circled back to Merla, who caught it and reattached it to the side of her head. Everyone laughed.

Since Shancus had been named in my honor, I guessed I'd better chip in with a verse of my own. Thinking quickly, I stood, cleared my throat, and chanted, "He's scaly and he's great, today he has turned eight, his name is Shancus — happy birthday!"

"Thanks, godfather." Shancus smirked. I wasn't really his godfather, but he liked to pretend I was — especially when it was his birthday and he was looking for a cool present!

A few others took turns singing birthday greetings to the snake-boy, then Evra stood and wrapped up the song with, "Despite the pranks you pull, your mom and I love you, pesky Shancus — happy birthday!"

There was lots of applause, then the women at the table shuffled over to hug and kiss Shancus. He pulled a mortified expression, but I could see he was delighted by the attention. His younger brother, Urcha, was jealous and sat a little way back from the table, sulking. Their sister, Lilia, was rooting through the piles of presents Shancus had received, seeing if there was anything of interest to a five-year-old girl.

Evra went to try and cheer up Urcha. Unlike Shancus, and Lilia, the middle Von child was an ordinary human and he felt he was the odd one out. Evra and Merla had a tough time making him feel special. I saw Evra slip a small present to Urcha, and heard him whisper, "Don't tell the others!" Urcha looked much happier after that. He joined Shancus at the table and tucked into a pile of small cakes.

I made my way over to where Evra was beaming at his family. "Eight years," I remarked, clapping Evra on his left shoulder (some of his scales had been sliced away from his right shoulder a long time ago, and he didn't like people touching him there). "I bet it feels like eight weeks."

"You don't know how right you are." Evra smiled. "Time flies when you have kids. You'll find out yourself one —" He stopped and grimaced. "Sorry. I forgot."

"Don't worry about it," I said. As a half-vampire, I was sterile. I could never have children. It was one of the drawbacks to being part of the clan.

"When are you going to show the snake to Shancus?" Evra asked.

"Later." I grinned. "I gave him a book earlier. He thinks that's his real present — he looked disgusted!

I'll let him enjoy the rest of the party, then hit him with the snake when he thinks the fun is over."

Shancus already owned a snake, but I'd bought a new one for him, larger and more colorful. Evra helped me choose it. His old snake would be passed on to Urcha, so both boys would have cause to celebrate tonight.

Merla called Evra back to the party — Lilia had got stuck in wrapping paper and needed to be rescued. I watched my friends for a minute or two, then turned my back on the festivities and walked away. I wandered through the maze of vans and tents of the Cirque Du Freak, coming to a halt near the Wolf Man's cage. The savage man-beast was snoring. I took a small jar of pickled onions out of my pocket and ate one, smiling sadly as I remembered where my taste for pickled onions had come from.

That memory led to others, and I found myself looking back over the years, recalling major events, remarkable triumphs, and sickening losses. The night of my blooding, when Mr. Crepsley pumped his vampiric blood into me. Slowly coming to terms with my appetite and powers. Sam Grest — the original pickled onion connoisseur. My first girlfriend, Debbie Hemlock. Learning about the vampaneze. The trek to

Vampire Mountain. My Trials, where I'd had to prove myself worthy of being a child of the night. Failing and running away. The revelation that a Vampire General — Kurda Smahlt — was a traitor, in league with the vampaneze. Exposing Kurda. Becoming a Prince.

The Wolf Man stirred and I walked on, not wanting to wake him. My mind continued to turn over old memories. Kurda telling us why he'd betrayed the clan — the Lord of the Vampaneze had arisen and stood poised to lead his people into war against the vampires. The early years of the War of the Scars, when I'd lived in Vampire Mountain. Leaving the safety of the fortress to hunt for the Vampaneze Lord, accompanied by Mr. Crepsley and Harkat. Meeting Vancha March, the third hunter — only he, Mr. Crepsley, or I could kill the Vampaneze Lord. Traveling with a witch called Evanna. Clashing with the Lord of the Vampaneze, unaware of his identity until afterwards, when he'd escaped with his protector, Gannen Harst.

I wanted to stop there — the next set of memories was the most painful — but my thoughts raced on. Returning to the city of Mr. Crepsley's youth. Running into Debbie again — an adult now, a teacher. Other faces from the past — R.V. and Steve Leopard. The former used to be an eco-warrior, a man who blamed me for the loss of his hands. He'd become a vampaneze and was part of a plot to lure my allies and me underground, where the Lord of the Vampaneze could kill us.

Steve was part of that plot too, though at first I thought he was on our side. Steve was my best friend when we were kids. We went to the Cirque Du Freak together. He recognized Mr. Crepsley and asked to be his assistant. Mr. Crepsley refused — he said Steve had evil blood. Later, Steve was bitten by Mr. Crepsley's poisonous tarantula. Only Mr. Crepsley could cure him. I became a half-vampire to save Steve's life, but Steve didn't see it that way. He thought I'd betrayed him and taken his place among the vampires. He became hell-bent on revenge.

Underground in Mr. Crepsley's city. Facing the vampaneze in a chamber Steve had named the Cavern of Retribution. Me, Mr. Crepsley, Vancha, Harkat, Debbie, and a police officer called Alice Burgess. A huge fight. Mr. Crepsley faced the man we thought was the Lord of the Vampaneze. He killed him. But then Steve killed Mr. Crepsley by knocking him into a pit of stakes. A gut-churning blow, made all the worse when Steve revealed the shocking truth — *he* was the real Lord of the Vampaneze!

I reached the last of the tents and stopped, gazing

around, half-dazed. We'd set up camp in an abandoned football stadium. It used to be the home field of the local football team, but they'd moved to a new, purpose-built stadium some years ago. The old stadium was due to be demolished — apartment blocks were to be built over the ruins — but not for several months yet. It was an eerie feeling, staring around at thousands of empty seats in the ghost stadium.

Ghosts . . . That put me in mind of my next, bizarre quest with Harkat, in what we now knew was a shade of the future. Once again I began to wonder if that ruined future world was unavoidable. Could I prevent it by killing Steve, or was it destined to come no matter who won the War of the Scars?

Before I got too worked up about it, someone stepped up beside me and said, "Is the party over?"

I looked around and saw the scarred, stitched-together grey-skinned face of Harkat Mulds. "No." I smiled. "It's winding down, but it hasn't finished yet."

"Good. I was afraid I'd miss it." Harkat had been out on the streets most of the day, handing out fliers for the Cirque Du Freak — that was one of his regular jobs every time we arrived at a new venue. He stared at me with his round, green lidless eyes. "How do you feel?" he asked.

"Strange. Worried. Unsure of myself."

"Have you been out there yet?" Harkat waved a hand at the town beyond the walls of the stadium. I shook my head. "Are you going to go, or do you plan . . . to hide here until we leave?"

"I'll go," I said. "But it's hard. So many years. So many memories." This was the real reason I was so fixed on the past. After all these years of travel, I'd returned home to the town where I was born and had lived all my human life.

"What if my family's still here?" I asked Harkat.

"Your parents?" he replied.

"And Annie, my sister. They think I'm dead. What if they see me?"

"Would they recognize you?" Harkat asked. "It's been a long time. People change."

"Humans do," I snorted. "But I've only aged four or five years."

"Maybe it wouldn't be a bad thing to . . . see them again," Harkat said. "Imagine their joy if they learned that . . . you were still alive."

"No," I said forcefully. "I've been thinking about that ever since Mr. Tall told me we were coming here. I *want* to track them down. It would be wonderful for me — but terrible for them. They buried me. They've done their grieving and have hopefully moved on with their lives. It wouldn't be fair to bring back all those old pains and torments."

"I'm not sure I agree with that," Harkat said, "but it's . . . your decision. So stay here with the Cirque. Lay low. Hide."

"I can't," I sighed. "This is my hometown. I've got an itch to walk the streets again, see how much has changed, look for old faces that I used to know. I want to find out what happened to my friends. The wise thing would be to keep my head down — but when did *I* ever do the wise thing?"

"And maybe trouble would find you . . . even if you did," Harkat said.

"What do you mean?" I frowned.

Harkat glanced around uneasily. "I have a strange feeling about . . . this place," he croaked.

"What sort of a feeling?" I asked.

"It's hard to explain. Just a feeling that this is . . . a dangerous place, but also the place where . . . we're meant to be. Something's going to happen here. Don't you sense it?"

"No — but my thoughts are all over the place right now."

"We've often discussed your decision to . . . stay with the Cirque," Harkat reminded me, making little of the many arguments we'd had about whether or not

I should leave and seek out the Vampire Generals. He believed I was hiding from my duty, that we should seek out the vampires and resume the hunt for the Vampaneze Lord.

"You're not starting that again, are you?" I groaned.

"No," he said. "The opposite. I now think you were right. If we hadn't stuck with the Cirque . . . we wouldn't be here now. And, as I said, I think we're . . . meant to be here."

I studied Harkat silently. "What do you think will happen?" I asked quietly.

"The feeling isn't that specific," Harkat said.

"But if you had to guess?" I pressed.

Harkat shrugged awkwardly. "I think we might run into . . . Steve Leonard, or find a clue that . . . points towards him."

My insides tightened at the thought of facing Steve again. I hated him for what he'd done to us, especially killing Mr. Crepsley. But just before he died, Mr. Crepsley warned me not to devote my life to hatred. He said it would twist me like Steve. So although I hungered for the chance to get even, I worried about it too. I didn't know how I'd react when I saw him again, whether I'd be able to control my emotions or give in to blind, hateful rage.

"You're frightened," Harkat noted.

"Yes. But not of Steve. I'm frightened of what *I* might do."

"Don't worry." Harkat smiled. "You'll be OK."

"What if . . ." I hesitated, afraid I'd jinx myself. But that was silly, so I came out with it. "What if Steve tries to use my family against me? What if he threatens my parents or Annie?"

Harkat nodded slowly. "I thought of that already. It's the sort of sick stunt I can . . . imagine him pulling."

"What will I do if he does?" I asked. "He already sucked Debbie into his insane plot to destroy me — not to mention R.V. What if —"

"Easy," Harkat soothed me. "The first thing is to find out if . . . they still live here. If they do, we can arrange protection . . . for them. We'll establish a watch around their house . . . and guard them."

"The two of us can't protect them by ourselves," I grunted.

"But we're not by ourselves," Harkat said. "We have many friends in . . . the Cirque. They'll help."

"You think it's fair to involve them?" I asked.

"They may already be involved," Harkat said. "Their destinies are tied to ours, I think. That may be another reason why you felt . . . you had to stay here."

Then he smiled. "Come on — I want to get to the party before . . . Rhamus scoffs all the cakes!"

Laughing, I put my fears behind me for a while and walked back through the campsite with Harkat. But if I'd known just how closely the destinies of my freakish friends were connected with mine, and the anguish I was steering them towards, I'd have about-faced and immediately fled to the other end of the world.

CHAPTER THREE

I DIDN'T GO EXPLORING THAT DAY. I stayed at the Cirque Du Freak and celebrated Shancus's birthday. He loved his new snake, and I thought Urcha was going to float away with joy when he found out Shancus's old snake was to be his. The party went on longer than expected. The table was loaded up with more cakes and pastries, and not even the ever-hungry Rhamus Twobellies could finish them off! Afterwards we prepared for that night's show, which went ahead smoothly. I spent most of the show in the wings, studying faces in the audience, looking for old neighbors and friends. But I didn't see anybody I recognized.

The next morning, while most of the Cirque folk were sleeping, I slipped out. Although it was a bright day, I wore a light jacket over my clothes, so I could pull the hood up and mask my face if I had to.

I walked rapidly, thrilled to be back. The streets had changed a lot — new shops and offices, many redecorated or redesigned buildings — but the names were the same. I ran into memories on every block. The shop where I bought my soccer boots. Mom's favorite clothes boutique. The theater where we'd taken Annie to her first film. The newsagent where I shopped for comics.

I wandered through a vast complex that used to be my favorite video arcade. It was under new ownership and had grown beyond recognition. I tried out some of the games, and smiled as I remembered how excited I'd get when I'd come here on a Saturday and blast away a few hours on the latest shoot-'em-up.

Moving away from the central shopping area, I visited my favorite parks. One was now a housing estate but the other was unchanged. I saw a groundskeeper tending to a bed of flowers — old William Morris, my friend Alan's grandfather. William was the first person from the past I'd seen. He hadn't known me very well, so I was able to walk right past him and study him up close without fear of being spotted.

I wanted to stop and chat with Alan's grandfather, and ask for news about Alan. I was going to tell him that I was one of Alan's friends, that I'd lost touch with him. But then I remembered that Alan was now an adult, not a teenager like me. So I walked on, silent, unobserved.

I was anxious to check out my old house. But I didn't feel ready — I trembled with nerves every time I thought about it. So I wandered through the center of town, past banks, shops, restaurants. I caught glimpses of half-remembered faces — clerks and waiters, a few customers — but nobody I'd known personally.

I had a bite to eat in a café. The food wasn't especially good, but it had been Dad's favorite place — he often brought me here for a snack while Mom and Annie were doing damage in the shops. It was nice to sit in the familiar surroundings and order a chicken and bacon sandwich, like in the old days.

After lunch, I strolled past my original school — a really eerie feeling! A new wing had been added, and there were iron railings around the perimeter, but apart from that it looked just the way I remembered. Lunch break was ending. I watched from underneath the shadows of a tree while the students filed back into class. I saw some teachers too. Most were new, but two caught my attention. One was Mrs. McDaid. She'd taught languages, mostly to older students. I'd had her for half a term when my regular teacher was on a leave of absence.

I'd been much closer to the other teacher — Mr. Dalton! I'd had him for English and history. He'd been my favorite teacher. He was chatting with some of his students as he entered class after lunch, and by their smiles I saw he was still as popular as ever.

It would have been great to catch up with Mr. Dalton. I was seriously thinking about waiting for school to finish, then going to see him. He'd know what had happened to my parents and Annie. I needn't tell him I was a vampire — I could say I had an anti-aging disease, which kept me looking young. Explaining away my "death" would be tricky, but I could cook up some story.

One thing held me back. A few years ago, in Mr. Crepsley's home city, I'd been branded a killer by the police, and my name and photo had been flashed all over the TV and newspapers. What if Mr. Dalton had heard about that? If he knew I was alive, and thought I was a murderer, he might alert the authorities. Safer not to take the risk. So I turned my back on the school and slowly walked away.

It was only then that it struck me that Mr. Dalton wouldn't be the only one who might have picked up on the "Darren Shan — serial killer!" hysteria. What if my parents had heard about it! Mr. Crepsley's city was in a different part of the world, and I wasn't sure how much news traveled between the two countries. But it was a possibility.

I had to sit down on a street bench while I considered that horrific possibility. I could only begin to imagine how shocking it would have been if, years after they'd buried me, Mom and Dad had spotted me on the news, under a caption branding me a killer. How had I never thought about it before?

This could be a real problem. As I'd told Harkat, I didn't intend to go see my family — too painful for everyone. But if they already knew I was alive, and were living with the misbelief that I was a killer, I'd have to set the record straight. But what if they *didn't* know?

I had to do some research. I'd passed a brand-new, ultra-modern library earlier that morning. Hurrying back to it, I asked a librarian for assistance. I said I was doing a school project and had to pick some local story from the last three years to write about. I asked to examine all the issues of the main local paper, as well as the national paper that my mom and dad used to read. I figured, if word of my exploits in Mr. Crepsley's city had spread this far, there'd be a mention of me in one of those two papers.

The librarian was happy to help. She showed me where the microfiche were stored, and how to use it. Once I'd got the knack of getting them up on-screen and scanning from one page to the next, she left me to my own devices.

I started with the earliest editions of the national paper, from a few months before I ran into trouble with the law. I was looking for any mention of Mr. Crepsley's city and the killers plaguing it. I made quick time, glancing only at the international sections. I found a couple of references to the murders — and they were both mocking! Apparently journalists here were amused by the vampire rumors that had swept the city, and the story was treated as light entertainment. There was a short piece in one issue, relaying the news that the police had caught four suspects, and then carelessly let all four escape. No names, and no mention of the people Steve had killed when he broke out.

I was relieved but angered at the same time. I knew the pain the vampaneze had brought to that city, the lives they'd destroyed. It wasn't right that such a grim story should be turned into the stuff of funny urban legends, simply because it happened in a city far away from where these people lived. They wouldn't have found it so amusing if the vampaneze had struck here!

I made a quick check on issues from the next few months, but the paper had dropped the story after news of the escape. I turned to the local paper. This was slower going. The main news was at the front, but local interest stories were scattered throughout. I had to check most of the pages of each edition before I could move on to the next.

Although I tried not to dwell on articles unrelated to me, I couldn't stop myself from skimming the opening paragraphs of the more interesting stories. It wasn't long before I was catching up with all the news — elections, scandals; heroes, villains; policemen who'd been highly commended, criminals who'd given the town a bad name; a big bank raid; coming in third in a national clean towns competition.

I saw photographs and read clips about several of my school friends, but one in particular stood out — Tom Jones! Tommy was one of my best friends, along with Steve and Alan Morris. We were two of the best soccer players in our class. I was the goal-scorer, leading the line up front, while Tommy was the goal-stopper, pulling off spectacular saves. I'd often dreamt of going on to be a professional soccer player. Tommy had taken that dream all the way.

There were dozens of photos and stories about him. Tom Jones (he'd shortened the "Tommy") was one of the best keepers in the world. Lots of articles poked fun at his name — there was also a famous singer called Tom Jones — but nobody had anything bad to say about Tommy himself. After working his way up through the amateur ranks, he'd signed for a foreign, world-famous club, and made a name for himself, eventually becoming captain of the national team.

In the most recent editions, I read how local soccer fans were buzzing with excitement at the prospect of a vital World Cup qualifier, which was being held in our town. It was Tommy's first game here in several years, and even non-soccer fans had been caught up in the hype. Organizers were expecting a huge, enthusiastic crowd on the day of the game.

Reading about Tommy brought a smile to my face — it was great to see one of my friends doing so well. The other good news was that there was no mention of me. Since this was quite a small town, I was sure word would have spread if anyone had heard about me in connection with the killings. I was in the clear.

But there was no mention of my family in the papers either. I couldn't find the name Shan anywhere. There was only one thing to do — I'd have to dig around for information in person by going back to the house where I used to live.

CHAPTER FOUR

THE HOUSE TOOK MY BREATH AWAY. It hadn't changed. Same color door, same style curtains, same small garden out back. As I stood gazing at it, gripping the top of the fence, I almost expected a younger version of myself to come bounding out the back door, clutching a pile of comics, on his way over to Steve's.

"May I help you?" someone asked behind me.

My head snapped round and my eyes cleared. I didn't know how long I'd been standing there, but by my white knuckles, I guessed it had been a few minutes at least. An elderly woman was standing close by, studying me suspiciously. Rubbing my hands together, I smiled warmly. "Just looking," I said.

"At what, precisely?" she challenged me, and I realized how I must appear to her — a rough-faced teenager, gazing intently into a deserted backyard, checking out the house. She thought I was a burglar casing the joint!

"My name's Derek Shan," I said, borrowing an uncle's first name. "My cousins lived here. In fact, they still might. I'm not sure. I'm in town to see some friends, and I thought I'd drop by and find out if my relatives were here or not."

"You're related to Annie?" the woman asked, and I shivered at the mention of the name.

"Yes," I said, fighting hard to keep my voice steady. "And Dermot and Angela." My parents. "Do they still live here?"

"Dermot and Angela moved away three or four years ago," the woman said. She stepped up beside me, at ease now, and squinted at the house. "They should have left sooner. That was never a happy house, not since their boy died." The woman looked sideways at me. "You know about that?"

"I remember my dad saying something," I muttered, ears turning red.

"I wasn't living here then," the woman said. "But I've heard all about it. He fell out of a window. The family stayed on, but it was a miserable place after that. I don't know why they stuck around so long. You can't enjoy yourself in a house of bitter memories."

CHAPTER FOUR

"But they did stay," I said, "until three or four years ago? And then moved on?"

"Yes. Dermot had a mild heart attack. He had to retire early."

"Heart attack!" I gasped. "Is he OK?"

"Yes." The woman smiled at me. "I said it was mild, didn't I? But they decided to move when he retired. Left for the coast. Angela often said she'd like to live by the sea."

"What about Annie?" I asked. "Did she go with them?"

"No. Annie stayed. She still lives here — her and her boy."

"Boy?" I blinked.

"Her son." The woman frowned. "Are you sure you're a relative? You don't seem to know much about your own family."

"I've lived abroad most of my life," I said truthfully.

"Oh." The woman lowered her voice. "Actually, I suppose it's not the sort of thing you talk about in front of children. How old are you, Derek?"

"Sixteen," I lied.

"Then I guess you're old enough. My name's Bridget, by the way."

"Hello, Bridget." I forced a smile, silently willing her to get on with the story.

"The boy's a nice enough child, but he's not really a Shan."

"What do you mean?" I frowned.

"He was born out of wedlock. Annie never married. I'm not even sure anyone except her knows who the father is. Angela claimed they knew, but she never told us his name."

"I guess lots of women choose not to marry these days," I sniffed, not liking the way Bridget was talking about Annie.

"True." Bridget nodded. "Nothing wrong with wanting the child but not the husband. But Annie was on the young side. She was just sweet sixteen when the baby was born."

Bridget was glowing, the way gossips do when they're telling a juicy story. I wanted to snap at her, but it was better to hold my tongue.

"Dermot and Angela helped raise the baby," Bridget continued. "He was a blessing in some ways. He became a replacement for their lost son. He brought some joy back into the house."

"And now Annie looks after him by herself?" I asked.

"Yes. Angela came back a lot during the first year,

for weekends and holidays. But now the boy's more independent, Annie can cope by herself. They get along as well as most, I guess." Bridget glanced at the house and sniffed. "But they could do with giving that old wreck a slap of paint."

"I think the house looks fine," I said stiffly.

"What do sixteen-year-old boys know about houses?" Bridget laughed. Then she bid me good day and went about her business. I was going to call her back, to ask when Annie would be home. But then I decided not to. Just as easy — and more exciting — to wait out here and watch for her.

There was a small tree on the other side of the road. I stood by it, hood up over my head, checking my watch every few minutes as though I was waiting to meet somebody. The street was quiet and not many people passed.

The day darkened and dusk set upon the town. There was a bite in the air but it didn't trouble me — half-vampires don't feel the cold as much as humans. I thought about what Bridget had said while I was waiting. Annie, a mother! Hard to believe. She'd been a kid herself the last time I saw her. From what Bridget said, Annie's life hadn't been the easiest. Being a mother at sixteen must have been rough. But it sounded like she had things under control now.

A light went on in the kitchen. A woman's silhouette passed from one side to the other. Then the back door opened and my sister stepped out. There was no mistaking her. Taller, with long brown hair, much plumper than she'd been as a girl. But the same face. The same sparkling eyes, and lips that were ready to turn up into a warmhearted smile at a moment's notice.

I stared at Annie as though in a trance. I wasn't able to tear my eyes away. I was trembling, and my legs felt like they were about to give way, but I couldn't turn my gaze aside.

Annie walked to a small washing line in the backyard, on which a boy's clothes were hanging. She blew into her hands to warm them, then reached up and took the clothes down, one garment at a time, folding each over the crook of her left arm.

I stepped forward and opened my mouth to call her name, all thoughts of not announcing myself forgotten. This was Annie — my sister! I *had* to talk to her, hold her again, laugh and cry with her, catch up on the past, ask about Mom and Dad.

But my vocal cords wouldn't work. I was choked up with emotion. All I managed was a thin croak. Closing my mouth, I walked across the road, slowing as I came to the fence. Annie had gathered all the clothes from the line and was returning to the kitchen.

CHAPTER FOUR

I gulped deeply and licked my lips. Blinked several times in quick succession to clear my head. Opened my mouth again —

— and stopped when a boy inside the house shouted, "Mom! I'm home!"

"About time!" Annie yelled in reply, and I could hear the love in her voice. "I thought I told you to bring in the clothes."

"Sorry. Wait a sec . . ." I saw the boy's shadow as he entered the kitchen and hurried over to the back door. Then he emerged, a chubby boy, fair-haired, very pleasant looking.

"Do you want me to take some of those?" the boy said.

"My hero," Annie laughed, handing half of the load over to the boy. He went in ahead of her. She turned to shut the door and caught a glimpse of me. She paused. It was quite dark. The light was behind her. She couldn't see me very well. But if I stood there long enough . . . if I called out to her . . .

I didn't.

Instead I coughed, pulled my hood tight around my face, spun, and walked away. I heard the door close behind me, and it was like the sound of a sharp blade slicing me adrift from the past.

Annie had her own life. A son. A home. Probably

a job. Maybe a boyfriend or somebody special. It wouldn't be fair if I popped up, opening old wounds, making her part of my dark, twisted world. She enjoyed peace and a normal life — much better than what I had to offer.

So I left her behind and slunk away quickly, through the streets of my old town, back to my real home — the Cirque Du Freak. And I sobbed my heart out every painful, lonely step of the way.

CHAPTER FIVE

I COULDN'T BEAR TO TALK to anybody that night. I sat by myself in a seat high up in the football stadium while the show was in progress, thinking about Annie and her child, Mom and Dad, all that I'd lost and missed out on. For the first time in years I felt angry with Mr. Crepsley for blooding me. I found myself wondering what life would be like if he'd left me alone, wishing I could go back and change the past.

But there was no point tormenting myself. The past was a closed book. I could do nothing to alter it, and wasn't even sure I would if I could — if I hadn't been blooded, I wouldn't have been able to tip the vampires off about Kurda Smahlt, and the entire clan might have fallen.

If I'd returned home ten or twelve years earlier, my

feelings of loss and anger might have been stronger. But I was an adult now, in all but looks. A Vampire Prince. I'd learned to deal with heartache. That wasn't an easy night. Tears flowed freely. But by the time I drifted off to sleep a few hours before dawn, I'd resigned myself to the situation, and knew there would be no fresh tears in the morning.

I was stiff with the cold when I awoke, but worked it off by jogging down the tiers of the stadium to where the Cirque was camped. As I was making for the tent I shared with Harkat, I spotted Mr. Tall. He was standing by an open fire, roasting sausages on a spit. He beckoned me over and threw a handful of sausages to me, then speared a fresh batch and stuck them over the flames.

"Thanks," I said, eagerly munching the piping-hot sausages.

"I knew you would be hungry," he replied. He looked at me steadily. "You have been to see your sister."

"Yes." It didn't surprise me that he knew. Mr. Tall was an insightful old owl.

CHAPTER FIVE

"Did she see you?" Mr. Tall asked.

"She saw me briefly, but I left before she got a good look."

"You behaved correctly." He turned the sausages over and spoke softly. "You are about to ask me if I will help protect your sister. You fear for her safety."

"Harkat thinks something's going to happen," I said. "He's not sure what. If Steve Leopard's part of it, he might use Annie to hurt me."

"He won't," Mr. Tall said. I was surprised by his directness — normally he was very cagey when it came to revealing anything about the future. "As long as you stay out of her life, your sister will be under no direct threat."

"What about *in*direct threat?" I asked warily.

Mr. Tall chuckled. "We are all under indirect threat, one way or another. Harkat is correct — this is a time and place of destiny. I can say no more about it, except leave your sister alone. She is safe that way."

"OK," I sighed. I wasn't happy about leaving Annie to fend for herself, but I trusted Hibernius Tall.

"You should sleep some more now," Mr. Tall said. "You are tired."

That sounded like a good plan. I wolfed another sausage, turned to leave, then stopped. "Hibernius," I said without facing him, "I know you can't tell me what's going to happen, but before we came here, you said I didn't have to come. It would have been better if I'd stayed away, wouldn't it?"

There was a long silence. I didn't think he was going to respond. But then, softly, he said, "Yes."

"What if I left now?"

"It is too late," Mr. Tall said. "Your decision to return set a train of events in motion. That train cannot be derailed. If you left now, it would only serve the purpose of the forces you oppose."

"But what if —" I said, turning to push the issue. But Mr. Tall had disappeared, leaving only the flickering flames and a stick speared with sausages lying on the grass next to the fire.

That evening, after I'd rested and enjoyed a filling meal, I told Harkat about my trip home. I also told him about my short conversation with Mr. Tall and how he'd urged me not to get involved with Annie.

"Then you were right," Harkat grunted. "I thought you should involve yourself with . . . your family again, but it seems I was wrong."

We were feeding scraps of meat to the Wolf Man,

part of our daily chores. We stood at a safe distance from his cage, all too aware of the power of his fearsome jaws.

"What about your nephew?" Harkat asked. "Any family resemblance?"

I paused, a large sliver of meat in my right hand. "It's strange, but I didn't think of him as that until now. I just thought of him as Annie's son. I forgot that also makes him my nephew." I grinned crookedly. "I'm an uncle!"

"Congratulations," Harkat deadpanned. "Did he look like you?"

"Not really," I said. I thought of the fair-haired, chubby boy's smile, and how he'd helped Annie bring in the washing. "A nice kid, from what I saw. Handsome, of course, like all the Shans."

"Of course!" Harkat snorted.

I was sorry I hadn't taken more notice of Annie's boy. I didn't even know his name. I thought about going back to ask about him — I could hang about and collar Bridget the gossip again — but dismissed the idea immediately. That was precisely the kind of stunt that could backfire and bring me to Annie's notice. Best to forget about him.

As we were finishing off, I saw a young boy watching us from behind a nearby van. He was studying us quietly, taking care not to attract attention. In the normal run of things, I'd have ignored him — children often came nosing around the Cirque site. But my thoughts were on my nephew and I found myself more interested in the boy than I would otherwise have been.

"Hello!" I shouted, waving at him. The boy's head instantly vanished behind the van. I would have left it, but moments later the boy stepped out and walked towards us. He looked nervous — understandable, since we were in the presence of the snarling Wolf Man — but he was fighting hard not to show it.

The boy stopped a few yards away and nodded curtly. "Hello," he mumbled. He was scrawny. He had dark blond hair and bright blue eyes. I put his age at somewhere in the region of ten or eleven, maybe a little bit older than Annie's kid, though there couldn't have been much of an age difference. For all I knew they might even be going to school together!

The boy said nothing after greeting us. I was thinking about my nephew and comparing this boy to him, so I said nothing either. Harkat finally broke the silence. "Hi," he said, lowering the mask he wore to filter out air, which was poisonous to him. "I'm Harkat."

CHAPTER FIVE

"Darius," the boy said, nodding at Harkat, not offering to shake hands.

"And I'm Darren." I smiled.

"You two are with the freak show," Darius said. "I saw you yesterday."

"You've been here before?" Harkat asked.

"A couple of times. I've never seen a freak show before. I tried buying a ticket but nobody will sell me one. I asked the tall guy — he's the owner, isn't he? — but he said it wasn't suitable for children."

"It is a bit on the gruesome side," I said.

"That's why I want to see it," he grunted.

I laughed, remembering what I'd been like at his age. "Tell you what," I said. "Why don't you walk around with us? We can show you some of the performers and tell you about the show. If you still want a ticket, maybe we can sort one out for you then."

Darius squinted at me suspiciously, then at Harkat. "How do I know I can trust you?" he asked. "You might be a pair of kidnappers."

"Oh, you have my word we won't . . . kidnap you," Harkat purred, treating Darius to his widest grin, displaying his grey tongue and sharp, pointed teeth. "We might feed you to the Wolf Man . . . but we won't kidnap you."

Darius yawned to show he wasn't impressed by the theatrical threat, then said, "What the hell, I've nothing better to do." Then he tapped his foot and raised an eyebrow impatiently. "Come on!" he snapped. "I'm ready!"

"Yes, master," I laughed, and led the harmless-looking boy on a tour of the Cirque.

CHAPTER SIX

WE WALKED DARIUS AROUND THE SITE and introduced him to Rhamus Twobellies, Cormac Limbs, Hans Hands, and Truska. Cormac was busy and didn't have time to show the boy how he could re-grow his limbs, but Truska sprouted a short beard for him, then sucked the hairs back into her face. Darius acted like he wasn't impressed, but I could see the wonder in his eyes.

Darius was strange. He didn't say much, and kept his distance, always a couple of yards away from Harkat and me, as though he still didn't trust us. He asked lots of questions about the performers and the Cirque Du Freak, which was normal. But he didn't ask anything about me, where I was from, how I'd come to join the show, or what my tasks involved. He didn't ask about Harkat either. The grey-skinned, stitched-together Little Person was like nothing most people had ever seen. It was common for newcomers to pump him for information. But Darius seemed uninterested in Harkat, as if he already knew everything about him.

He also had a way of staring at me oddly. I'd catch him looking at me, when he thought my attention was elsewhere. It wasn't a threatening look. There was just something about the flickering of his eyes that for some reason unsettled me.

Harkat and I weren't hungry, but when we passed one of the open campfires and saw a pot of bubbling soup, I heard Darius's stomach rumble. "Want to eat?" I asked.

"I'm having dinner when I go home," he said.

"How about a snack, to keep you going?"

He hesitated, then licked his lips and nodded quickly. "But just a small bowl of soup," he snapped, as though we meant to force-feed him.

While Darius was downing the soup, Harkat asked if he lived nearby.

"Not far off," he answered vaguely.

"How did you find out . . . about the show?"

Darius didn't look up. "A friend of mine — Oggy Bas — was here. He was going to take some seats — we often come here when we want seats or railings. It's easy to get in and nobody cares what we take. He saw the circus tent and told me. I thought it was an ordinary circus until I came exploring yesterday."

"What sort of a name is Oggy Bas?" I asked.

"Oggy's short for Augustine," Darius explained.

"Did you tell Oggy what the Cirque Du . . . Freak really was?" Harkat asked.

"Nah," Darius said. "He's got a big mouth. He'd tell everybody and they'd all come. I like being the only one who knows about it."

"So you're a boy who knows how to keep a secret," I chuckled. "Of course, the downside is that since nobody knows you're here, if we *did* kidnap you or feed you to the Wolf Man, nobody would know where to look."

I was joking, but Darius reacted sharply. He half-bolted to his feet, dropping the unfinished bowl of soup. Acting instinctively, I snatched for the bowl, and with my vampire speed I caught it before it hit the ground. But Darius thought I meant to strike him. He threw himself backwards and roared, "Leave me alone!"

I took a surprised step back. The other people around the fire were gaping at us. Harkat's green eyes were on Darius, and there was more than just surprise in his expression — he looked wary too.

"Easy," I half-laughed, lowering the bowl, then

raising my hands in a gesture of friendship. "I'm not going to hurt you."

Darius sat up. He was blushing angrily. "I'm OK," he mumbled, getting to his feet.

"What's wrong, Darius?" Harkat asked quietly. "Why so edgy?"

"I'm OK," Darius said again, glaring at Harkat. "I just don't like people saying stuff like that. It's not funny, creatures like you making threats like that."

"I didn't mean it," I said, ashamed for having frightened the boy. "How about I get a ticket to tonight's show for you, to make up for scaring you?"

"I ain't scared," Darius growled.

"Of course you aren't." I smiled. "But would you like a ticket anyway?"

Darius pulled a face. "How much are they?"

"It's free," I said. "Courtesy of the house."

"OK then." That was as close as Darius got to saying thanks.

"Would you like one for Oggy too?" I asked.

"No," Darius said. "He wouldn't come. He's a scaredy-cat. He doesn't even watch horror movies, not even the really old and boring ones."

"Fair enough," I said. "Wait here. I'll be back in a couple of minutes."

I tracked down Mr. Tall. When I told him what I

wanted, he frowned and said all the tickets for tonight's show had been sold. "But surely you can find a spare one somewhere," I laughed. There was always lots of space in the aisle and it was usually not a problem to stick in a few extra chairs.

"Is it wise, inviting a child to the show?" Mr. Tall asked. "Children tend to fare unfavorably here. Yourself, Steve Leonard, Sam Grest." Sam was a boy who'd had a fatal run-in with the Wolf Man. He was the first person I'd drunk blood from. Part of his spirit — not to mention his taste for pickled onions! — still lived on within me.

"Why mention Sam?" I asked, confused. I couldn't remember the last time Mr. Tall had made a reference to my long-dead friend.

"No reason in particular," Mr. Tall said. "I just think this is a dangerous place for children." Then he produced a ticket out of thin air and handed it to me. "Give it to the boy if you wish," he grumbled, as if I'd squeezed an inconvenient favor out of him.

I walked back slowly to Darius and Harkat, wondering why Mr. Tall had behaved in such a curious manner. Had he been trying to warn me not to let Darius get too closely involved with the Cirque De Freak? Was Darius like Sam Grest, eager to leave home and travel around with a band of magical performers? By inviting him to the show, was I setting him up for a fall like Sam's?

I found Darius standing where I'd left him. He didn't look like he'd moved a muscle. Harkat was on the other side of the fire, keeping a green eye on the boy. I hesitated before giving Darius his ticket. "What do you think of the Cirque Du Freak?" I asked.

"It's OK." He shrugged.

"How would you feel about joining?"

"What do you mean?" he asked.

"If there was an opening, and you had the chance to leave home, would —"

"No way!" he snapped before I finished.

"You're happy at home?"

"Yes."

"You don't want to travel around the world?"

"Not with you creeps."

I smiled and gave him the ticket. "That's OK then. The show starts at ten. Will you be able to come?"

"Of course," Darius said, pocketing the ticket without looking at it.

"What about your parents?" I asked.

"I'll go to bed early, then sneak out," he said, and giggled slyly.

"If you're caught, don't tell them about us," I warned him.

"As if!" he snorted, then waved sharply and left. He looked at me one final time before he passed out of sight, and again there was something odd about his gaze.

Harkat walked around the fire and stared after the boy.

"A strange kid," I commented.

"More than just strange," Harkat murmured.

"What's wrong?" I asked.

"I don't like him," Harkat said.

"He was a bit sullen," I agreed, "but lots of kids his age are like that. I was that way myself when I first joined the Cirque Du Freak."

"I don't know." Harkat's eyes were full of doubt. "I didn't buy his story about his . . . friend, Oggy. If he's such a scaredy-cat, what was he . . . doing exploring up here by himself?"

"You're getting suspicious in your old age," I laughed.

Harkat shook his head slowly. "You didn't pick up on it."

"What?" I frowned.

"When he accused us of threatening him, he said . . . 'creatures like you.'"

"So?"

Harkat smiled thinly. "I'm quite obviously *not*

human. But what tipped him off to the fact . . . that *you* aren't either?"

A sudden chill ran through me. Harkat was right — the boy had known more about us than he should have. And I realized now what it was about Darius's gaze that had disturbed me. When he thought I wasn't looking, his eyes kept going to the scars on my fingertips, the standard marks of a vampire — like he knew what they meant!

CHAPTER SEVEN

HARKAT AND I WEREN'T SURE what to make of Darius. It seemed unlikely that the vampaneze would recruit children. But there was the twisted mind of their leader, Steve Leopard, to take into account. This could be one of his evil, hate-fueled games. We decided to take the boy to one side when he came to the show, and pump him for information. We wouldn't resort to torture or anything so drastic — just try to scare a few answers out of him.

We were supposed to help the performers get ready for the show, but we told Mr. Tall we were busy and he assigned our tasks to other members of the troupe. If he knew about our plans for Darius, he didn't say so.

There were two entrances to the big top. Shortly

before the audience started to arrive, Harkat and I each took up a position close to one of the entry points, where we could watch for Darius. I was still worried about being recognized by somebody who'd known me in the past, so I stood in the shadows beside the entrance, disguised in a set of Harkat's blue robes, the hood pulled up to hide my face. I watched silently as the early birds trickled in, handing their tickets to Jekkus Flang (Mr. Tall was on the other entrance). With every third or fourth customer, Jekkus threw their ticket into the air, then launched a knife at it, spearing it through the middle and pinning it to a nearby post.

As the trickle of people turned into a steady stream, and Jekkus pinned more and more tickets to the pole, the tickets and knives took on the outline of a hanged man. People chuckled edgily when they realized what Jekkus was doing. A few paused to commend him on his knife-throwing skills, but most hurried past to their seats, some glancing backwards at the figure of the hanged man, perhaps wondering if it was an omen of things to come.

I ignored the hanged man — I'd seen Jekkus perform this trick many times before — and focused on the faces in the crowd. It was hard to note everybody who passed in the crush, especially short people. Even if Darius entered this way, there was no guarantee I'd spot him.

Towards the end of the line, as the last members of the audience were filing in, Jekkus gave a gasp of surprise and abandoned his post. "Tom Jones!" he shouted, bounding forward. "What an honor!"

It was the town's famous goalkeeper, Tom Jones — my old school friend!

Tommy smiled awkwardly and shook Jekkus's hand. "Hi," he coughed, looking around to see if anyone else had noticed him. Apart from those nearest us, nobody had — all eyes were fixed on the stage, as everyone awaited the start of the show.

"I've seen you play!" Jekkus enthused. "You're awesome! Do you think we'll win tomorrow? I wanted to get a ticket, but they were sold out."

"It's a big match," Tommy said. "I could try to get one for you, but I don't think —"

"That's OK," Jekkus interrupted. "I'm not trying to shake you down for free tickets. Just wanted to wish you good luck. Now, speaking of tickets, could I see yours?"

Tommy gave his ticket to Jekkus, who asked if Tommy would sign it for him. Tommy obliged and

Jekkus pocketed the ticket, beaming happily. He offered to find a seat for Tommy near the front, but Tommy said he was happy to sit at the back. "I don't think it would be good for my image if word got out that I came to shows like this," he laughed.

As Tommy made his way to one of the few free seats, I breathed a sigh of relief — he hadn't seen me. The luck of the vampires was on my side. I waited a few more minutes, until the final stragglers had been admitted, then crept out as Jekkus closed off the entrance. I linked up with Harkat.

"Did you see him?" I asked.

"No," Harkat said. "You?"

"No. But I saw an old friend." I told him about Tom Jones.

"Could it be a setup?" Harkat asked.

"I doubt it," I said. "Tommy wanted to come to the Cirque Du Freak the last time it was in town. He's here for the match tomorrow. He must have heard about the show and picked up a ticket — easy when you're a celebrity."

"But isn't it a bit too coincidental that . . . he's here the same time as us?" Harkat persisted.

"He's here because our national team's a World Cup qualifier," I reminded Harkat. "Steve couldn't have engineered that — even the Lord of the Vampaneze has his limits!"

"You're right," Harkat laughed. "I really am getting paranoid!"

"Let's forget about Tommy," I said. "What about Darius? Could he have got in without us seeing him?"

"Yes," Harkat said. "It was impossible to identify . . . everyone who entered. A child could have easily . . . passed without us noticing."

"Then we've got to go inside and look for him," I said.

"Steady on." Harkat stopped me. "Although your friend Tommy's being here is most likely . . . nothing to worry about, let's not tempt fate. If you go in, your hood might slip . . . and he might see you. Leave it to me."

While I waited outside, Harkat entered the tent and patrolled the aisles, checking the faces of every audience member as the show got under way. More than half an hour passed before he emerged.

"I didn't see him," Harkat said.

"Maybe he isn't able to sneak away from home," I said.

"Or maybe he sensed we were . . . suspicious of him," Harkat said. "Either way, we can't do anything except . . . keep watch the rest of the time we're here. He might come sneaking around . . . by day again."

Although it was anticlimactic, I was glad Darius hadn't shown. I hadn't been looking forward to threatening the boy. It was better this way, for all concerned. And the more I thought about it, the more ridiculous our reaction seemed. Darius had certainly known more about us than any child should, but maybe he'd simply read the right books or found out about us on the Internet. Not many humans know about the true marks of a vampire, or that Little People exist, but the truth (like they used to say on that famous TV show) is out there! There were any number of ways a clued-in kid could have found out the facts about us.

Harkat wasn't as relaxed as I was, and he insisted we stay outside the entrances until the show finished, in case Darius turned up late. There was no harm in being cautious, so I kept watch throughout the rest of the show, listening to the gasps, screams, and applause of the people inside the tent. I slipped away a few minutes before the end and collected Harkat. We hid in a van as the crowd poured out, and only emerged when the final excited customer had left the stadium.

We gathered with most of the performers and backstage crew in a tent behind the big top for the

CHAPTER SEVEN

post-show party. There wasn't a celebration after each performance, but we liked to let our hair down every once in a while. It was a hard life on the road, driving long distances, working doggedly, keeping a low profile so as not to attract attention. It was good to chill out now and then.

There were a few guests in the tent — police officers, council officials, wealthy businessmen. Mr. Tall knew how to grease the right palms, to make life easy for us.

Our visitors were particularly interested in Harkat. The normal audience members hadn't seen the grey-skinned Little Person. This was a chance for the special guests to experience something different, which they could boast about to their friends. Harkat knew what was expected of him and he let the humans examine him, telling them a bit about his past, politely answering their questions.

I sat in a quiet corner of the tent, munching a sandwich, washing it down with water. I was getting ready to leave when Jekkus Flang pushed his way through a knot of people and introduced me to the guest he'd just led into the tent. "Darren, this is the world's best goalkeeper, Tom Jones. Tom, this is my good friend and fellow workmate, Darren Shan."

I groaned and closed my eyes. So much for the luck

of the vampires! I heard Tommy gasp with recognition. Opening my eyes, I forced a smile, stood, shook Tommy's hand — his eyes were bulging out of his head — and said, "Hello, Tommy. It's been a long time. Can I get you something to drink?"

CHAPTER EIGHT

TOMMY WAS ASTONISHED to see me alive when I'd been declared dead and buried eighteen years earlier. Then there was the fact that I only looked a handful of years older. It was almost too much for him to comprehend. For a while he listened to me talk, nodding weakly, not taking anything in. But eventually his head cleared and he focused on what I was saying.

I spun him a far-fetched but just about believable tale. I felt bad, lying to my old friend, but the truth was stranger than fiction — it was simpler and safer this way. I said I had a rare disease that prevented me from aging normally. It was discovered when I was a child. The doctors gave me five or six years to live. My parents were devastated by the news, but since we could do nothing to prevent it, we told no one and tried to lead a normal life for as long as we could.

Then the Cirque Du Freak came to town.

"I ran into an extraordinary physician," I lied. "He was traveling with the Cirque, making a study of the freaks. He said he could help me, but I'd have to leave home and travel with the Cirque — I'd need constant monitoring. I talked it over with my parents and we decided to fake my death, so I could leave without arousing suspicions."

"But for heaven's sake, why?" Tommy exploded. "Your parents could have left with you. Why put everyone through so much pain?"

"How would we have explained it?" I sighed. "The Cirque Du Freak is an illegal traveling show. My parents would have had to give up everything and go undercover to be with me. It wouldn't have been fair to them, and it would have been dreadfully unfair to Annie."

"But there must have been some other way," Tommy protested.

"Maybe," I said. "But we didn't have much time to think it over. The Cirque Du Freak was only in town for a few days. We discussed the proposal put forward by the physician and accepted it. I think the fact that I'm still alive all these years later, against all medical odds, justifies that decision."

Tommy shook his head uncertainly. He'd grown up

to be a very large man, tall and broad, with huge hands and bulging muscles. His black hair was receding prematurely — he'd be bald in a few more years. But despite his physical presence, his eyes were soft. He was a gentle man. The idea of letting a child fake his death and be buried alive was repulsive to him.

"What's done is done," I said. "Maybe my parents should have searched for another way. But they had my best interests at heart. Hope was offered and they seized it, regardless of the terrible price."

"Did Annie know?" Tommy asked.

"No. We never told her." I guessed Tommy had no way of contacting my parents directly, to check out my story, but he could have gone to Annie. I had to sidetrack him.

"Not even afterwards?" Tommy asked.

"I talked about it with Mom and Dad — we keep in touch and meet up every few years — but we never felt the time was right. Annie had her own problems, having a baby so young."

"That *was* tough," Tommy agreed. "I was still living here. I didn't know her very well, but I heard all about it."

"That must have been just before your soccer career took off," I said, leading him away from talk about me. We discussed his career after that, some of the big matches he'd been involved in, what he planned to do when he retired. He wasn't married but he had two kids from a previous relationship.

"I only get to see them a couple of times a year and during the summer," he said sadly. "I hope to move to where they live when I quit soccer, to be closer to them."

Most of the performers, crew, and guests had departed by this stage. Harkat had seen me talking with Tommy and made a sign asking if I wanted him to stick around. I signaled back that I was OK and he'd left with the others. A few people still sat and talked softly in the tent, but nobody was near Tommy and me.

Talk turned to the past and our old friends. Tommy told me Alan Morris had become a scientist. "Quite a famous one too," he said. "He's a geneticist — big into cloning. A controversial area, but he's convinced it's the way forward."

"As long as he doesn't clone himself!" I laughed. "One Alan Morris is enough!"

Tommy laughed too. Alan had been a close friend of ours, but he could be a bit of a pain at times.

"I've no idea what Steve's up to," Tommy said, and the laughter died on my lips. "He left home at sixteen. Ran off without a word to anyone. I've spoken to him on the phone a few times, but I've only seen him once since then, about ten years ago. He returned home for a few months when his mother died."

"I didn't know she was dead," I said. "I'm sorry. I liked Steve's mom."

"He sold off the house and all her effects. He shared an apartment with Alan for a while. That was before . . ." Tommy stopped and glanced at me oddly. "Have *you* seen Steve since you left?"

"No," I lied.

"You don't know anything about him?"

"No," I lied again.

"Nothing at all?" Tommy pressed.

I forced a chuckle. "Why are you so concerned about Steve?"

Tommy shrugged. "He got into some trouble the last time he was here. I thought you might have heard about it from your parents."

"We don't discuss the past," I said, elaborating on the lie I'd concocted. I leaned forward curiously. "What did Steve do?" I asked, wondering if it was in any way linked to his vampaneze activities.

"Oh, I don't rightly remember," Tommy said, shifting uncomfortably — he was lying. "It's old history. Best not to bring it up. You know what Steve was like, always in one form of trouble or another."

"That's for sure," I muttered. Then my eyes narrowed. "You said you've talked to him on the phone?"

"Yeah. He rings every so often, asks what I'm up to, says nothing about what he's doing, then hangs up!"

"When was the last time he rang?"

Tommy thought about it. "Two, maybe three years ago. A long time."

"Do you have a contact number for him?"

"No."

Too bad. I'd thought for a moment that Tommy might be my path back to Steve, but it seemed he wasn't.

"What's the time?" Tommy asked. He looked at his watch and groaned. "If my manager finds out how late I've been out, I'll catch hell! Sorry, Darren, but I really have to go."

"That's OK." I smiled, standing to shake his hand. "Maybe we could meet up again after the match?"

"Yeah!" Tommy exclaimed. "I'm not traveling with the team — I'm staying here for the night, to see some relatives. You can come to the hotel after the game and . . . Actually, how'd you like to come see me play?"

"At the World Cup qualifier?" My eyes lit up. "I'd love to. But didn't I hear you telling Jekkus the tickets were sold out?"

CHAPTER EIGHT

"Jekkus?" Tommy frowned.

"The guy with the knives — your number one fan."

"Oh." Tommy grimaced. "I can't give away tickets to all my fans. But family and friends are a different story."

"I wouldn't be sitting near anyone who knew me, would I?" I asked. "I don't want the truth about me going any further — Annie might hear about it."

"I'll get you a seat away from the others," Tommy promised. Then he paused. "You know, Annie's not a girl anymore. I saw her a year ago, the last time I was here to visit family. She struck me as being very levelheaded. Maybe it's time to tell her the truth."

"Maybe." I smiled, knowing I wouldn't.

"I really think you should," Tommy pressed. "It would be a shock, like it was for me, but I'm sure she'd be delighted to know you're alive and well."

"We'll see," I said.

I walked Tommy out of the tent, through the campsite and stadium tunnels to where his car was parked. I bid him good night at the car, but he stopped before getting in and stared at me seriously. "We must talk some more about Steve tomorrow," he said.

My heart skipped a beat. "Why?" I asked as casually as I could.

"There are things you should know. I don't want to

get into them now — it's too late — but I think . . ." He trailed off into silence, then smiled. "We'll talk about it tomorrow. It might help you make up your mind about some other things."

And on that cryptic note he said farewell. He promised to send over a ticket in the morning, gave me his hotel name and cell number, shook my hand one last time, got into his car, and drove away.

I stood outside the walls of the stadium a long while, thinking about Tommy, Annie, and the past — and wondering what he'd meant when he said we needed to talk some more about Steve.

CHAPTER NINE

WHEN I TOLD HARKAT about the match, he reacted with automatic suspicion. "It's a trap," he said. "Your friend is an ally of . . . Steve Leonard."

"Not Tommy," I said with absolutely certainty. "But I have a feeling he might in some way be able to direct us to him, or set us on his trail."

"Do you want me to come with . . . you to the match?" Harkat asked.

"You wouldn't be able to get in. Besides," I laughed, "there'll be tens of thousands of people there. In a crowd like that, I think I'll be safe!"

The ticket was delivered by courier and I set off in good time for the match. I arrived an hour before kickoff. A huge crowd milled around outside the stadium. People were singing and cheering, decked out in our country's colors, buying drinks, hot dogs, and burgers from the street vendors. Troops of police kept a close watch on the situation, making sure rival fans didn't clash.

I mingled for a while, strolling around the stadium, relishing the atmosphere. I bought a hot dog, a match program, and a hat with Tommy's picture on it, sporting the slogan, "He's not unusual!" There were lots of hats and badges dedicated to Tommy. There were even CDs by the singer Tom Jones, with photos of Tommy taped across the covers!

I took my seat twenty minutes before kickoff. I had a great view of the floodlit pitch. My seat was in the middle of the stadium, just a few rows behind the dugouts. The teams were warming up when I arrived. I got a real buzz out of seeing Tommy in one of the goals, stopping practice shots. To think one of my friends was playing in a World Cup qualifier! I'd come a long way since childhood and put most of my human interests behind me. But my love of soccer came flooding back as I sat, gazing down at Tommy, and I felt a ball of pure childish excitement build in the pit of my stomach.

The teams left the pitch to get ready for kickoff,

then re-emerged a few minutes later. All the seats in the stadium had been filled and there was a huge cheer as the players marched out. Most people stood up, clapping and hollering. The ref tossed a coin to decide which way the teams would play, then Tommy and the other captain shook hands, the players lined up, the ref blew his whistle, and the game got under way.

It was a brilliant game. Both teams went all out for the win. Tackles flew in fast and hard. Play shifted from one end to the other, both sides attacking in turn. There were lots of chances to score. Tommy made some great saves, as did the other goalkeeper. A couple of players blasted wide or over the bar from good positions, to a chorus of jeers and groans. After forty-three minutes, the teams seemed like they'd be tied at halftime. But then there was a quick break, a defender slipped, a forward had a clear shot at a goal, and he sent the ball flying into the left corner of the net, past the outstretched fingers of a flailing Tom Jones.

Tommy and his teammates looked dejected as they trudged off at halftime, but the home fans kept on singing, "One-nil down, two-one up, that's the way to win the cup!"

I went to get a drink but the size of the line was frightening — the more experienced fans had slipped out just before the halftime whistle. I walked around to stretch my legs, then returned to my seat.

Although they were a goal down, Tommy's team looked more confident when they came out after the break. They attacked from the start of the half, knocking their opponents off the ball, pushing them back, driving hard for a goal. The game grew heated and three players got yellow cards within the first quarter of an hour. But their newfound hunger was rewarded in the sixty-fourth minute when they scored a scrappy goal from a corner to tie the score.

The stadium erupted when our team scored. I was one of the thousands who leapt from their seats and punched the air with joy. I even joined in with the song to the silenced fans of the other country's team, "You're not singing, you're not singing, you're not singing anymore!"

Five minutes later, I was chanting even louder when, from another corner, we scored again to go two-one up. I found myself hugging the guy next to me — a total stranger! — and jumping up and down with glee. I could hardly believe I was behaving this way. What would the Vampire Generals say if they saw a Prince acting so ridiculously!

The rest of the game was a tense affair. Now that they were a goal down, the other team had to attack in search of an equalizer. Tommy's teammates were forced farther back inside their own half. There were dozens of desperate defensive tackles, lots of free kicks, more yellow cards. But they were holding out. Tommy had to make a few fairly easy saves, but apart from that his goal wasn't troubled. With six minutes to go, the win looked safe.

Then, in virtually an action replay of the first goal, a player slipped free of his defender and found himself in front of the goal, with only Tommy to beat. Once again the ball was struck firmly and accurately. It streaked towards the lower left corner of the net. The striker turned away to celebrate.

But he'd reacted too soon. Because this time, somehow, Tommy got down and across, and managed to get a few fingers to the ball. He only barely connected, but it was enough to tip the ball out around the goalpost.

The crowd went wild! They were chanting Tommy's name and singing, "It's not unusual, he's the greatest number one!" Tommy ignored the songs and stayed focused on the corner, directing his defenders. But the save had sapped the other team of their spirit, and though they kept coming forward for the final few minutes, they didn't threaten to score again.

When the whistle blew, Tommy's team wearily embraced each other, then shook their opponents' hands and swapped jerseys. After that they saluted their fans, acknowledging their support. We were all on our feet, applauding, singing victory songs, a lot of them about the incredible Tom Jones.

Tommy was one of the last players to leave the field. He'd swapped his jersey with his opposite number, and the pair were walking off together, discussing the game. I roared Tommy's name as he came level with the dug-outs, but of course he couldn't hear me over the noise of the crowd.

Just as Tommy was about to vanish down the tunnel to the locker rooms, a commotion broke out. I heard angry yells, then several sharp bangs. Most of the people around me didn't know what was happening. But I'd heard these sounds before — gunfire!

I couldn't see down the tunnel from where I was, but I saw Tommy and the other goalkeeper stop, confused, then back away from the tunnel entrance. I immediately sensed danger. "Tommy!" I screamed, then knocked aside the people nearest me and forced my way down towards the pitch. Before I got there, a steward reeled out of the tunnel, blood pouring from his face. When the people in front of me saw that, they panicked. Turning, they pushed away from the field, halting my advance and forcing me back.

CHAPTER NINE

As I struggled to break free, two figures darted out of the tunnel. One was a shaven-headed, shotgun-toting vampet with a disfigured, half-blown-away face. The other was a bearded, purple-skinned, crazy vampaneze with silver and gold hooks instead of hands.

Morgan James and R.V.!

I screamed with fresh fear when I saw the murderous pair, and shoved aside everyone around me, drawing on the full extent of my vampire powers. But before I could bruise a way through, R.V. homed in on his target. He bounded past the dugouts, ignored the players, coaching staff, and stewards on the field, and bore down on a startled Tom Jones.

I don't know what flashed through Tommy's mind when he saw the burly purple monster streaking towards him. Maybe he thought it was a practical joke, or a weird fan coming to hug him. Either way, he didn't react, raise his hands to defend himself, or turn to run. He just stood, staring dumbly at R.V.

When R.V. reached Tommy, he pulled back his right hand — the one with the gold hooks — then jabbed the blades sharply into Tommy's chest. I froze, feeling Tommy's pain from where I was trapped in the crowd. Then R.V. jerked his hooked hand back, shook his head with insane delight, and retreated down the tunnel, following Morgan James, who fired his gun to clear a path.

On the field, Tommy stared stupidly down at the red, jagged hole in the left side of his chest. Then, with almost comical effect, he slid gracelessly to the ground, twitched a few times, and lay still — the terrible, unmistakable stillness of the dead.

CHAPTER TEN

BURSTING FREE OF THE CROWD, I stumbled onto the field. Those around me were staring at the fallen goalkeeper, paralyzed with shock. My first instinct was to run to Tommy. But then my training kicked in. Tommy had been killed. I could grieve for him later. Right now I had to focus on R.V. and Morgan James. If I hurried after them, I might catch up before they got away.

Tearing my gaze away from Tommy, I ducked down the tunnel; past the players, staff, and stewards who had yet to recover their senses. I saw more shot-up bodies but didn't stop to check whether they were living or dead. I had to be a vampire, not a human. A killer, not a carer.

I raced down the tunnel until it branched off in two directions. Left or right? I stood, panting, scanning the corridors for clues. Nothing to my left, but there was a small red mark on the wall to my right — blood.

I picked up speed again. A voice at the back of my mind whispered, "You have no weapons. How will you defend yourself?" I ignored it.

The corridor led to a locker room, where most members of the winning team had gathered. The players weren't aware of what had happened on the field. They were cheering and singing. The corridor branched again here. The path to the left led back towards the field, so I took another right turn, praying to the gods of the vampires that I'd chosen correctly.

A long sprint. The corridor was narrow and low-ceilinged. I was panting hard, not from exertion but from sorrow. I kept thinking about Tommy, Mr. Crepsley, Gavner Purl — friends I'd lost to the vampaneze. I had to fight the sorrow, or it would overwhelm me, so I thought about R.V. and Morgan James instead.

R.V. was once an eco-warrior. He'd tried to free the Wolf Man at the Cirque Du Freak. I'd stopped him but not before the Wolf Man had bitten his hands off. R.V. fled, survived, and blamed me for his misfortune. Some years later, he was discovered by Steve Leopard. Steve told the vampaneze to blood him, and the pair plotted my downfall. R.V. had been in the Cavern of

Retribution when Mr. Crepsley was killed. That was the last time I'd seen him.

Morgan James was an ex–police officer. A vampet, one of the humans the vampaneze had recruited. Like the other vampets, he dressed in a brown shirt and black pants, shaved his head, painted circles of blood around his eyes, and had a "V" tattooed above each ear. Since he hadn't been blooded, he was free to use missile-firing weapons such as guns. Vampaneze, like vampires, swear an oath when they're blooded not to use such weapons. James had also been in the Cavern of Retribution. During the battle he was shot, and the left side of his face had been torn into fleshy strips by the bullet.

A treacherous, deadly pair. Again I found myself wondering what I'd do if I caught up with them — I didn't have any weapons! But again I ignored that problem and concentrated on the chase.

The end of the corridor. A door swinging ajar. Two police officers and a steward lying slumped against the wall — dead. I cursed R.V. and Morgan James, and swore revenge.

I kicked the door wide open and ducked out. I was at the rear of the stadium, the quietest part of the area, backing onto a housing project. The police who had been posted out here had been attracted to the sides of the stadium — there was some kind of a disturbance at the front, no doubt timed to tie in with the assault.

Ahead of me I saw R.V. and Morgan James enter the projects. By the time the police turned their attention this way, the killers would be gone. I started after them. Stopped. Hurried back inside the stadium and frisked the dead police officers. No guns, but both had been carrying batons. I took the clubs, one for each hand, then fled after my prey.

It was dark in the projects, especially after the brightness of the stadium. But I had the extra-sharp vision of a half-vampire, so I was able to negotiate my way without any problems. The road branched off at regular intervals, one or two buildings per stretch. I paused briefly at each junction, looking left and right. No sign of R.V. and Morgan James. Forward again.

I wasn't sure if they knew I was following. I assumed they knew I was at the game, but they might not have counted on me being the first to break out of the stadium and pursue them. The element of surprise *might* be on my side, but I warned myself not to count on it.

I came to the last junction. Left or right? I stood in the road, head twisting one way, then the other. I couldn't see anyone. I'd lost them! Should I take a direction at random or backtrack and —

CHAPTER TEN

There was a soft screeching sound to my left — a blade scraping against a wall. Then someone hissed, "Quiet!"

I turned. There was a tiny alley between two buildings, the source of the noise. The nearest streetlights had been smashed. The only illumination came from across the road. I had a bad feeling about this — the screech and hiss had been far too convenient — but I couldn't back off now. I advanced.

I stopped a couple of yards from the alley and edged out into the middle of the road. My knuckles were white from gripping the batons. I came into gradual sight of the alley. Nobody near the dark mouth. The alley ran back only five or six yards, and even in the poor light I could see all the way to the rear wall. Nobody was there. I breathed out shakily. Maybe my ears had been playing tricks. Or else the sound had been a TV or radio. What should I do now? I was back where I'd been moments before, no idea which way to —

Something moved in the alley, low down on the floor. I stiffened and lowered my sights. And now I saw them, crouched where it was darkest, one hugging either wall, practically invisible in the shadows.

The figure to my left chuckled, then stood — R.V. I raised the baton in my left hand defensively. Then the figure to my right rose, and Morgan James stepped forward, bringing up his shotgun, pointing it at me. I began to raise the baton in my right hand against him, then realized how worthless it would be if he fired.

I took another step back, meaning to run, when a voice spoke from the darkness behind R.V. "No guns," it said softly. Morgan James immediately lowered the barrel of his shotgun.

I should have run, but I couldn't, not without putting a face to that voice. So I stood my ground, squinting, as a third shape formed and stepped out from behind R.V. It was Gannen Harst, the prime protector of the Lord of the Vampaneze.

Part of me had expected this, and instead of panicking, I experienced something close to relief. The waiting was over. Whatever destiny had in store for me, it started here. One final encounter with the Vampaneze Lord. At the end of it, I'd kill him — or he'd kill me. Either way was better than the waiting.

"Hello, Gannen," I said. "Still hanging out with madmen and scum, I see."

Gannen Harst bristled but didn't reply. "Lord," he said instead, and a fourth ambusher stepped out from behind Morgan James, more familiar than any of the others.

CHAPTER TEN

"Good to see you again, Steve," I said cynically as the grey-haired Steve Leopard slid into view. I was partly focused on Gannen Harst, R.V., and Morgan James — but mostly on Steve. I was judging the gap between us, wondering what sort of damage I could do if I hurled my truncheons at him. I didn't care about the other three — killing the Vampaneze Lord was my first priority.

"He doesn't look surprised to see us," Steve remarked. He hadn't stepped out as far as Gannen Harst, and was protected by the body of Morgan James. I might be able to hit him from this angle — but it was a very big *might*.

"Let me have him," R.V. snarled, taking a step towards me. The last time I'd seen him, he'd been wearing red contact lenses, and had painted his skin purple, to look more like a vampaneze. But his eyes and skin had changed naturally over the past two years, and though his coloring was slight in comparison to a mature vampaneze, it was genuine.

"Stay where you are," Steve said to R.V. "We can all have a slice of him later. Let's finish the introductions first. Darius."

From behind Steve, the boy called Darius stepped out. He was wearing green robes, like Steve. He was shivering, but his face was set sternly. He was holding a large arrow-gun, one of Steve's inventions. It was pointed at me.

"Have you started blooding children now?" I growled disgustedly, still waiting for Steve to move out a little more, ignoring the threat of the boy's arrow-gun.

"Darius is an exception," Steve said, smiling. "A most worthy ally and a valuable spy."

Steve took a half-step towards the boy. This was my chance! I began to draw my right hand back, careful not to give my intentions away, totally focused on Steve. Another second or two and I could make my play . . .

Then Darius spoke.

"Shall I shoot him now, Dad?"

DAD?

"Yes, son," Steve replied.

SON?

While my brain spun and whirled like a dervish, Darius steadied his aim, gulped, pulled the trigger, and shot a steel-tipped arrow straight at me.

CHAPTER ELEVEN

THE ARROW STRUCK ME HIGH in my right shoulder, knocking me backwards. I roared with agony, grabbed the shaft of the arrow, and pulled. The shaft broke off in my hand, leaving the head stuck deep in my flesh.

For a moment the world around me turned red. I thought I was going to pass out. But then the crimson haze faded and the road and houses swam back into focus. Over the sound of my pained panting, I heard footsteps coming towards me. Sitting up — grinding my teeth together to fight back a wave of fresh pain — I saw Steve leading his small band in for the kill.

I'd let go of the batons when I fell. One had rolled away, but the other was close by. I snatched for it and for the shaft of the arrow — the splintered end could be used as a crude dagger. When Gannen Harst saw this, he stepped in front of Steve. "Fan out!" he commanded R.V. and Morgan James. They swiftly obeyed. The boy, Darius, was behind Steve. He looked sick. I don't think he'd ever shot anyone before.

"Keep back!" I hissed, waving my pitiful weapons at them.

"Make us," R.V. giggled.

"Uhr'd luhk tuh shee im truhy!" said Morgan James, who could only speak in a slur since his accident.

"We won't let him try anything," Gannen Harst said quietly. He hadn't drawn his sword yet, but his right hand was hanging purposefully by his scabbard. "He's a dangerous foe, even injured — don't forget that."

"You think too much of the boy," Steve purred, looking at me over his protector's shoulder. "He won't even be able to get up with a wound like that."

"Won't I?" I snorted, and pushed myself to my feet just to spite him. A red curtain descended for the second time, but again it passed after a couple of seconds. When my sight cleared, I saw Steve grinning wickedly — he'd goaded me to my feet on purpose, to string more entertainment out of me.

Waving the arrow shaft around at the four men, I backed away. Each step was torture, the pain in my right shoulder flaring up at the slightest movement. It was clear that I couldn't get very far, but Gannen was taking no chances. He sent R.V. to my left and James to my right, blocking my route in both directions.

I stopped, weaving heavily on my feet, woozily trying to formulate a plan. I knew only Steve could kill me — Des Tiny had predicted doom for the vampaneze if anybody other than their Lord killed any of the vampire hunters — but the others could hold me down for him.

"Let's finish him off quickly," Gannen Harst said, finally drawing his sword. "He is at our mercy. Let's not waste time."

"Take it easy," Steve chuckled. "I want to see him bleed a bit more."

"And if he bleeds to death from your son's arrow?" Gannen snapped.

"He won't," Steve said. "Darius shot exactly where I trained him to." Steve glanced back at the boy and caught his troubled look. "Are you OK?"

"Yes," Darius croaked. "I just didn't think it would be so . . . so . . ."

"Bloody," Steve said. He nodded understandingly. "You did good work tonight. You don't have to watch the rest if you don't want to."

"How did . . . *you* end up with . . . a son?" I gasped, playing for time, hoping an escape would present itself.

"A long, twisted story," Steve said, facing me again. "One I'll delight in telling you before I drive a stake through your heart!"

"You got that . . . the wrong way round." I laughed bleakly. "*I'll* be the one doing . . . the killing tonight."

"Optimistic to the last." Steve smirked. He cocked a devilish eyebrow at me. "How did Tommy die — with dignity, or like that squealing pig Crepsley?"

At that, something snapped inside me. I screamed a foul insult at Steve and, without thinking, hurled my baton at him. With blind luck, it struck his forehead and he dropped with a startled grunt.

Gannen Harst instinctively swung away from me, to check on his Lord. As soon as he made his move, I made mine. Jumping at Morgan James, I lashed out with the arrow shaft. He took a quick step back to avoid being speared. As he did, I smashed into him with my wounded right shoulder. I howled with pain as the arrowhead was forced deeper into my flesh, but my ploy worked — James toppled over.

The path ahead was momentarily clear. I stumbled forward, grasping my right shoulder with my left hand, pressing hard around the hole where the arrowhead was buried, trying to stem the flow of blood, weeping with agony. Behind me I heard Steve shout, "I'm OK! Chase him! Don't let him get away!"

If I hadn't been injured, I might have had enough of a head start on them. But I could manage nothing faster than a slow jog. It was only a matter of seconds before they'd catch up with me.

As I lurched away, my pursuers hot on my heels, a door to one of the buildings on my left opened and a large man stuck his head out. "What's all the noise about?" he shouted angrily. "Some of us are trying to —"

"Help!" I screamed on impulse. "Murder!"

The man threw the door all the way open and stepped out. "What's going on?" he yelled.

I looked back at Steve and the others. They'd come to a halt. I had to make the most of their confusion. "Help!" I screamed at the top of my lungs. "Killers! They've shot me! Help!"

Lights began flicking on in the neighboring buildings, and curtains were swished back. The man who'd come out started towards me. Steve sneered, reached over his shoulder, produced an arrow-gun, and fired at the man. Gannen Harst knocked the arrow-gun aside just before Steve fired, so the arrow whizzed wide of its mark. But the man had seen Steve's intent and he ran back inside his house before he could be fired upon again.

"What are you doing?" Steve furiously challenged Gannen Harst.

"We must get out of here!" Gannen shouted.

"Not without killing him!" Steve yelled, jerking his arrow-gun at me.

"Then kill him, quick, and let's go!" Gannen responded.

Steve stared at me, eyes filled with hatred. Behind him, R.V. and Morgan James were looking on with hungry longing, eager to see me die. Darius was farther removed from the gang — I couldn't tell if he was watching or not.

Steve raised his arrow-gun, took a couple of steps closer, trained his sights on me, then . . .

. . . lowered it, unfired. "No," he said sullenly. "This is too easy. Too fast."

"Don't be foolish!" Gannen roared. "You have to kill him! This is the predicted fourth encounter. You must do it now, before —"

"I'll do what I please!" Steve yelled, turning on his mentor. For a moment I thought he meant to attack his closest ally. But then he got ahold of himself and smiled tightly. "I know what I'm doing, Gannen. I can't kill him this way."

"If not now, then when?" Gannen snarled.

"Later," Steve said. "When the time is right. When I can torment him at my leisure and make him feel the pain I felt when he betrayed me and pledged himself to Creepy Crepsley."

"And Mr. Tiny's prophecy?" Gannen hissed.

"Stuff it!" Steve smirked. "I'll create my own destiny. That mug in the rain boots doesn't rule my life."

Gannen's red eyes were ablaze with rage. This was madness. He wanted Steve to kill me, to settle the War of the Scars once and for all. He would have argued the point, but more doors were opening and people were poking their heads out. Gannen realized they were in danger of attracting too much unwanted attention. He shook his head, then grabbed Steve, spun him away from me, and pushed him back the way they'd come, ordering R.V. and Morgan James to retreat.

"Catch you later, vampire-gator!" Steve laughed, waving at me as Gannen shepherded him away.

I wanted to respond with a suitable insult, but I lacked the strength. Besides, I had to get out of there as quickly as Steve and his gang. If the people came out and found me, I'd be in major trouble. It would mean the police, hospital, recognition, and arrest — I was still a wanted fugitive. The general public here might not know about the alleged killer Darren Shan, but I was sure the police did.

Turning my back on the emerging humans, I staggered to the end of the block, where I rested a moment, leaning against a wall. I wiped sweat from my forehead and tears from my eyes, then checked the hole in my shoulder — still bleeding. There was no time to examine it further. People were spilling out onto the street. It wouldn't be long before news of the killings at the stadium trickled through. Then they'd be on their phones to the police, telling them all about the disturbance.

Pushing myself away from the wall, I stumbled left and started down a path that would hopefully lead me away from the projects. I tried to jog but it was too painful. I slowed to the fastest walk I could manage, bleeding with every step I took, head ringing, desperately wondering how far I could struggle on before I collapsed from loss of blood or shock.

CHAPTER TWELVE

I CLEARED THE HOUSING PROJECTS a few minutes later. In the distance police sirens screamed like banshees in the night. The stadium would be their first priority, but once word reached them of the scuffle in the projects, units would be sent to investigate.

As I stood bent over, panting for breath, I studied the path I'd taken and saw little puddles of blood marking my course — a clear trail for anyone who followed. If I was to progress any farther undetected, I'd have to do something about my wound.

I examined the hole. There was a tiny bit of shaft sticking out of it, attached to the arrowhead. I took hold of the light piece of wood, closed my eyes, bit down hard, and pulled.

"Charna's guts!"

I fell back, shivering, fingers twitching, mouth

opening and shutting rapidly. For maybe a minute, I knew only pain. The buildings around me could have collapsed and I wouldn't have noticed.

Gradually the pain abated and I was able to study the wound again. I hadn't managed to pull the head out, but I'd drawn it closer towards the hole, plugging it up. Blood still oozed out but it wasn't flowing steadily like it had been. That would have to do. Tearing a long strip off my shirt, I balled it up and pressed it over the wound. After a few deep breaths, I got to my feet. My legs were shaking like a newborn lamb's, but they held. I made sure I wasn't dripping blood, then resumed my sluggish flight.

The next ten or fifteen minutes passed in a slow, agonized blur. I had enough sense left to keep moving, but I wasn't able to take note of street names or plot a course back to the Cirque Du Freak. All I knew was that I couldn't stop.

I kept to the sides of streets and alleys, so I could grab a fence for support or lean against a wall to rest. I didn't pass many people. Those I did pass ignored me. That surprised me, even in my dazed state, until I realized how I must look. A teenager, reeling along the path, head bowed, body crooked over, moaning softly — they thought I was drunk!

CHAPTER TWELVE

Eventually I had to stop. I was at the end of my rope. If I didn't sit down and rest, I'd drop in the middle of the street. Luckily I was close to a dark alley. I fell into it and crawled away from the streetlights, deep into welcome shadows. I stopped beside a large black garbage can, sat up against the wall by which it was set, and dragged my legs in.

"Just . . . a short . . . rest," I wheezed, laying my head on my knees, wincing at the pain in my shoulder. "A few . . . minutes . . . and then I can . . ."

I got no further. My eyelids fluttered shut and I passed out, at the mercy of any who happened to chance upon me.

My eyes opened. It was later, darker, colder. I felt like I was encased in a block of ice. I tried lifting my head, but even that small effort proved too much for me. I blacked out again.

The next time I awoke, I was choking. Some stinging liquid was being forced down my throat. For a confused moment I thought I was a raw half-vampire again, and that Mr. Crepsley was trying to force me to drink human blood. "No!" I mumbled, slapping at the hands holding my head. "Not gonna . . . be like you!"

"Hold him still!" someone grunted.

"It's not that easy," the person holding me complained. "He's stronger than he looks." Then I felt a body pressing down on mine, and a voice whispered in my ear, "Steady, kid. We're only trying to help."

My head cleared slightly and I stopped struggling. Blinking, I tried to focus on the faces of the men around me, but it was either too dark or my sight was clouded with pain. "What . . . are you?" I gasped, meaning were they friends or foes.

The man holding me must have misheard my question, and thought I'd asked *who* were they. "I'm Declan," he said. "This is Little Kenny."

"Open wide," Little Kenny said, pressing the rim of a bottle to my lips. "This is cheap and nasty, but it'll warm you up."

I drank reluctantly, unable to argue. My stomach filled with a sickening fire. When Little Kenny took the bottle away, I leaned my head back against the wall and groaned. "What time . . . is it?" I asked.

"We don't bother with watches," Declan chuckled.

"But it's late, maybe one or two in the morning." He took hold of my chin, turned my head left and right, then picked at the strip of shirt that was stuck to my shoulder with dried blood.

"Ow!" I yelped.

Declan released me immediately. "Sorry," he said. "Does it hurt much?"

"Not . . . as much . . . as it did," I muttered. Then my head began to swim and I half-blacked-out again. When I recovered, the two men were huddled together a few feet away, discussing what to do with me.

"Leave him," I heard Little Kenny hiss. "He can't be more than sixteen or seventeen. He's no good to us."

"Every person matters," Declan disagreed. "We can't afford to be picky."

"But he's not one of *us,*" Little Kenny said. "He probably has a family and home. We can't start recruiting normal people, not until we're told."

"I know," Declan said. "But there's something different about him. Did you see his scars? And he didn't get that wound fighting on the playground. We should take him back with us. If the ladies choose not to keep him, we can get rid of him easily enough."

"But he'll know where we are!" Little Kenny objected.

"The shape he's in, I doubt he even knows what town this is!" Declan snorted. "He's got more things to worry about than marking the route we take."

Little Kenny grumbled something I couldn't hear, then said, "OK, but don't forget it was your choice, not mine. I'm not taking the blame for this."

"Fine," Declan said, and returned to my side. He rolled my eyelids all the way up and I got my first clear look at him. He was a large, bearded man, dressed in shabby clothes, covered in grime — a tramp. "Kid," he said, snapping his fingers in front of my eyes. "You awake? Do you know what's going on?"

"Yes." I glanced over at Little Kenny and saw that he was also a tramp.

"We're taking you back with us," Declan said. "Can you walk?"

I assumed that they meant to take me to a mission house or homeless shelter. That wasn't as preferable as the Cirque Du Freak, but it was better than a police station. I wet my lips and locked gazes with Declan. "No . . . police," I moaned.

Declan laughed. "See?" he said to Little Kenny. "I told you he was our kind of people!" He took hold of my left arm and told Little Kenny to take my right. "This will hurt," he warned me. "You ready for it?"

"Yes," I said.

They pulled me to my feet. The pain in my shoulder flared back into life, my brain ignited with fireworks, and my stomach lurched. Doubling over, I threw up on the alley floor. Declan and Little Kenny held me while I vomited, then hauled me up.

"Better?" Declan asked.

"No!" I gasped.

He laughed again, then shuffled around, dragging me with him, so we were facing the entrance of the alley. "We'll carry you as best we can," Declan said. "But try to use your legs — it'll make life easier for all of us."

I nodded to show I understood. Declan and Little Kenny linked hands behind my back, put their other hands on my chest to support me, then led me away.

Declan and Little Kenny were a strange pair of guardian angels. They encouraged me along with a series of curses, pushes, and pulls, kicking my feet every so often to goad me into short bursts of self-momentum. We rested every few minutes, leaning against walls or lampposts, Declan and Little Kenny panting almost as hard as I was. They obviously weren't accustomed to this much exercise.

Even though it was the middle of the night, the town was abuzz. Word of the stadium slaughter had spread, and people had taken to the streets in outrage. Police cars passed us regularly, sirens blaring, flash-lights glaring.

We marched in plain view of the police and angry citizens, but nobody took any notice of us. With Declan and Little Kenny holding me, I looked like the third of a trio of drunk tramps. One policeman did stop and shout at us to get the hell off the streets — hadn't we heard what happened?

"Yes, sir," Declan mumbled, half-saluting the police-man. "Going home right now. Don't suppose you could arrange a lift for us?"

The policeman snorted and turned away. Declan chuckled, then led us on again. When we were out of earshot, he said to Little Kenny, "Any idea what all the fuss is about?"

"Something to do with soccer, I think," Little Kenny said.

"How about you?" Declan asked me. "Do you know what people are up in arms about?"

I shook my head. Even if I'd wanted to tell them the truth, I couldn't have. The pain was worse than ever. I had to keep my teeth ground tightly together to stop myself from screaming out loud.

We carried on walking. I half-hoped I'd black out again, to numb myself to the pain. I didn't even care that Declan and Little Kenny would probably dump me in a gutter to die, rather than drag my deadweight body along. But I stayed awake, if not entirely alert, and managed to swing my legs into action when prompted.

I had no idea where I was being taken, and I wasn't able to raise my head to mark the way. When we finally came to a halt in front of an old brown-faced building, Little Kenny darted forward to open a door. I tried looking up to see what the number was. But even that was beyond me, and I could only stare at the ground through half-closed eyes as Declan and Little Kenny dragged me inside and laid me on a hard wooden floor.

Little Kenny stayed with me, keeping watch, as Declan went upstairs. They'd laid me on my left side, but I rolled over onto my back and stared up at the ceiling. I could feel my last sparks of consciousness flickering out. As I watched, my eyes played tricks and I imagined the ceiling was shimmering, like seawater in a light breeze.

I heard Declan coming back with somebody. He was talking quickly and quietly. I tried turning my head to see whom he was bringing, but the scene on the ceiling was too captivating to turn away from. Now I was imagining boats, sails filled with the breeze, circling the sea-ceiling above me.

Declan stopped by my side and examined me. Then he stepped back and the person with him bent over to look. That's when I knew I was really losing my grip on reality, because in my delirium I thought the person was Debbie Hemlock, my ex-girlfriend. I smiled weakly at the ludicrous thought of running into Debbie here. Then the woman standing over me exclaimed, "Darren! Oh my —"

And then there was only darkness, silence, and dreams.

CHAPTER THIRTEEN

"OW! IT'S HOT!" I winced.

"Don't be a baby." Debbie smiled, pressing a spoon of steaming hot soup to my lips. "It's good for you."

"Not if it scalds my throat," I grumbled. I blew on the soup to cool it, swallowed, then smiled at Debbie as she dipped the spoon into the bowl again. Harkat stood guard by the door. Outside I could hear Alice Burgess talking with one of their street people. I felt incredibly safe as I lay there, sipping soup, like nothing in the world could harm me.

It had been five days since Declan and Little Kenny rescued me. The first few days passed in a haze. I'd been racked with pain and a high fever, senses in disarray, subject to nightmares and delusions. I kept thinking Debbie and Alice were imaginary. I'd laugh when they talked to me, convinced my brain was playing tricks.

But as the fever broke and my senses returned, the faces of the women remained constant. When I finally realized it really was Debbie, I threw my arms around her and hugged her so hard, I almost fainted again!

"Would you like some soup?" Debbie asked Harkat.

"No," Harkat replied. "Not hungry."

I asked Debbie to fetch Harkat and Mr. Tall even before she'd told me what she and Alice were doing here. When my worried friend arrived — Mr. Tall didn't come — I told him about Steve and his gang, and about Steve being Darius's father. Harkat's round green eyes almost doubled in size when he heard that. I wanted him to leave and contact the Vampire Generals, but he refused. He said he had to stay to protect me, and wouldn't go until I was fit again. I argued the point, but it was no good. He hadn't left the room since then, except for the occasional bathroom break.

Debbie spooned the last of the soup into my mouth, wiped around my lips with a napkin, and winked. She'd hardly changed in the two years we'd been apart. The same lush dark skin, beautiful brown eyes, full lips, and tightly cropped hair. But she was more physically developed than before. She was leaner, more muscular, and she moved with a fighter's fluid grace. Her eyes were always alert. She was never totally at ease, ready to respond to any threat at an instant's notice.

The last time we'd met, Debbie and Alice had been on their way to Vampire Mountain. They were troubled by the rise of the vampaneze and shaven-headed vampets — they thought they'd turn on humanity next if they won the War of the Scars. They decided that the vampires should create their own human force to combat the threat of the gun-wielding vampets. They planned to offer their services to the Generals, and hoped to put together a small army to battle the vampets, leaving the vampires free to tackle the vampaneze.

I didn't think the Generals would accept their proposal. Vampires have always distanced themselves from humans, and I thought they'd reject Debbie and Alice automatically. But Debbie told me that Seba Nile — the quartermaster of Vampire Mountain, and an old friend of Mr. Crepsley's and mine — had spoken on their behalf. He said times had changed and the Generals needed to change with them. Vampires and vampaneze had sworn an oath never to use missile-firing weapons, but the vampets hadn't. Many vampires were being shot by the shaven-headed curs. Seba said something had to be done about it, and this was their chance to fight the vampets on level terms.

As the oldest living vampire, Seba was greatly respected. Upon his recommendation Debbie and Alice were accepted, albeit with reluctance. For several months they'd trained in the vampire ways, mostly at the hands of my old task master, Vanez Blane. The blind vampire taught them to fight and think as creatures of the night. It wasn't easy — the ever-wintry Vampire Mountain was a hard place to survive if you lacked the hot blood of the vampires — but they'd clung to each other for support and stuck with it, earning the admiration even of those Generals who'd greeted them with suspicion.

Ideally they'd have trained for several years, learning the ways of vampire warfare. But time was precious. The vampets were growing in number, taking part in more and more battles, killing more and more vampires. Once Debbie and Alice had covered the basics, they set out with a small band of Generals to assemble a makeshift army. Debbie told me Seba and Vanez longed to come with them, for one last taste of adventure in the outside world. But they served the clan best on Vampire Mountain, so they stayed, loyal servants to the end.

The door to my room opened and Alice stepped in. Alice Burgess used to be a police chief inspector and she looked even more warrior-like than Debbie. She was taller and broader, with more pronounced muscles. Her white hair was cut ultra-short, and though she was extremely light-skinned, there was nothing soft about her complexion. She looked as pale and deadly as a snowstorm.

"The police are searching the neighborhood," Alice said. "They'll be here in an hour or less. Darren will have to hide again."

The building was old and had once been used as a church by a shady preacher. He'd created a couple of secret rooms, almost impossible to find. They were stuffy and uncomfortable, but safe. I'd stayed in one of them three times already, to avoid the police searches that had been in full flow since the massacre at the football stadium.

"Any word from Vancha?" I asked, sitting up and pushing the bedcovers back.

"Not yet," Alice said.

As the other surviving hunter, Vancha March was the only person apart from me who could freely kill Steve. Debbie and Alice didn't have a direct line to the Prince, but they'd equipped a number of the younger, more forward-thinking Generals with cell phones. One would get word to Vancha about the situation here — eventually. I just prayed it wouldn't be too late.

Recruiting an army had proved a lot harder than it

sounded. No vampire knew for sure how the vampaneze had put the vampets together, but we could imagine their recruiting strategy — find weak-willed, wicked people, then bribe them with promises of power. "Join us and we'll teach you how to fight and kill. We'll blood you when the time is right and make you stronger than any human. As one of us, you'll live for centuries. Anything you wish for can be yours."

Debbie and Alice faced a much harder task. They needed good people who were willing to fight on the side of right, who recognized the threat the vampets and their master posed, who wished to avert the prospect of living in a world where a band of killers dominated the night. Crooked, grasping, evil-hearted people were easy to find. Honest, concerned, self-sacrificing people were harder to come by.

They found a few, among police and soldiers — Alice had lots of contacts from her time on the force — but nowhere near enough to counter the threat of the vampets. For half a year they made little or no progress. They were beginning to think it was a waste of time. Then Debbie saw the way forward.

The vampaneze were on the increase. As well as recruiting the vampets, they were blooding more vampaneze assistants than normal, driving up their numbers in a bid to win the War of the Scars by means of force. Since they were more active than usual, they needed to drink more blood, to keep up their energy levels. And when vampaneze drank blood, they killed.

So where were all the bodies?

Vampaneze had survived for six hundred years by feeding cautiously, never killing too many people in any one area, carefully hiding the bodies of their victims. There weren't many of them — never more than three hundred before the War of the Scars — and they were spread across the world. It was relatively easy to keep their presence a secret from humanity.

But now they were on the increase, feeding in groups, killing hundreds of humans every month. There was no way such a drain on humanity could have passed unnoticed by the general public — unless those they fed on weren't officially part of that public.

Tramps. Hobos. Vagrants. Mankind had dozens of names for homeless people, those without careers, houses, families, or security. Many names — but not a lot of interest. Homeless people were a nuisance, a problem, an eyesore. Whether "ordinary" people felt pity or disgust for them, whether they handed over change when they saw someone begging or walked straight by, one thing united most humans — they knew homeless people existed, but very few took any real notice of them. Who in any town or city could say how many homeless people were living on the streets? Who'd know if those numbers started to drop? Who'd care?

The answer — almost nobody. Except the homeless people themselves. *They'd* know something was wrong. The homeless would listen, pitch in, and fight. If not for the vampires, then for themselves — they were victims of the War of the Scars, and stood to lose big-time if the vampaneze were triumphant.

So Debbie, Alice, and their small band of Generals took their recruiting speeches to the corners of the world most humans know nothing about. They went out on the streets, into homeless shelters and mission churches, down alleys lined with rough beds made of cardboard boxes and wads of newspapers. They moved freely among the people of this subworld, facing suspicion and danger, spreading their message, in search of allies.

And they found them. There was a grapevine among the homeless, similar to that of the vampire clan. Though most lacked phones, they kept in touch with one another. It was amazing how fast a rumor could travel, and wherever Alice and Debbie went, they found people who'd heard about the murders and knew they were under attack, even though they had no idea who their attackers were.

Debbie and Alice told the street people about the vampaneze. They encountered skepticism to begin with, but the vampires with them backed them up, demonstrating their powers. In a couple of cities they helped the street folk track down vampaneze and kill them. Word spread rapidly, and over the last several months thousands of street people across the world had pledged themselves to the vampire cause. Most hadn't been trained yet. For now they were serving as eyes and ears, watching for vampaneze, passing on word of their movements.

They'd also chosen a name — *vampirites.*

Harkat helped me out of bed and I hobbled from my room, down the corridor and stairs to the ground floor, where the hidden rooms were located. Alice came with us, to ensure all was in order. We passed Declan along the way. He was on the phone to another nearby vampirite stronghold, warning them of the police search.

The Generals with Debbie and Alice left them eventually, to resume the fight against the vampaneze — all hands were needed in the War of the Scars. A couple kept in touch, meeting up with them every month or two, monitoring their progress. But most of the time the ladies of the shadows — as the vampirites referred to them — traveled alone, choosing places where the vampaneze were active, recruiting fervently.

They'd come to my hometown two weeks ago. There'd been many reports of vampaneze here, and a band of vampirites had already formed to combat them. Debbie and Alice came to raise morale, and also to spread awareness among the street folk. That task accomplished, they'd planned to move on soon. Then I'd turned up, beaten and bleeding, and their plans changed.

I rubbed my right shoulder as I shuffled to the secret room. Alice had removed the arrowhead and stitched me up. The wound had healed cleanly, but it still stung like crazy, and I was a long way from full recovery.

Alice and Harkat moved the furniture that helped mask the entrance to the hidden room at the rear of the house. Then Alice pressed a secret panel and a section of wall slid back to reveal a cramped cell. There was a very dim light set in one of the walls.

"They searched the house thoroughly last time," Alice reminded me, checking that the jug beside the mattress on the floor was filled with water. "You could be in for another long stay."

"I'll be fine," I said, lying down.

"Hold on!" I heard Debbie shout, as Alice was

about to close the section of wall on me. She came hurrying to the entrance, carrying a small bag. "I've been waiting until you were strong enough to give this to you. It will help pass the time."

"What is it?" I asked, taking the bag.

"You'll see," Debbie replied, blowing me a kiss and stepping back as the cell was closed off. I waited a minute for my eyes to adjust to the dim light, then reached inside the bag and pulled out several notepads bound together by a rubber band. I broke into a smile — my diary! I'd forgotten it entirely. Now that I cast my thoughts back, I recalled handing the notepads to Alice before leaving with Harkat two years earlier.

I slipped the rubber band off the pads, thumbed through the copy on top, then paused, upended the diary, and went back eighteen years to before I sneaked out to the Cirque Du Freak and met Mr. Crepsley. Within minutes I was adrift in the past, and the hours flew by as I focused on my scrawled writing, aware of nothing else.

CHAPTER FOURTEEN

ONCE I GOT THE ALL CLEAR, I returned to my bedroom and spent the next couple of days bringing my diary up to date. I'd soon filled out the most recent notepad, so Debbie brought me fresh writing material. I wrote all about my adventures with Harkat in the barren wasteland that seemed to be the world of the future. I described my fears, that the world might face destruction regardless of who won the War of the Scars, and that I might be in some way linked to the fall of mankind. I told about discovering Harkat's true identity and returning home. A quick rundown of our recent travels with the Cirque Du Freak. Then the latest cruel chapter, in which Tommy died and I learned that Steve had a son.

I hadn't thought much about Tommy since that night. I knew the police were scouring the city in search of his killers, and that R.V. and Morgan James had killed eight others and wounded many more in the stadium. But I didn't know what the general public made of the murders, or if I'd been identified as a suspect — maybe Steve was setting me up to take the blame for this.

I asked Debbie to bring me all the local papers from the last few days. There were poor pictures of R.V. (full-vampaneze couldn't be photographed, but R.V.'s molecular system must not have changed yet) and Morgan James, but none of me. There was a brief mention of the incident outside the stadium, when I'd been attacked, but the police didn't seem to place much importance on it or link it with the stadium murders.

"Were you close to him?" Debbie asked, tapping a photo of a smiling Tommy Jones. She was sitting on the end of my bed, watching me while I read the papers. She'd been spending a lot of time with me during my recovery, nursing me, chatting with me, telling me about her life.

"We were good friends when we were kids," I sighed.

"Do you think he knew about Steve or the vampaneze?" Debbie asked.

"No. He was an innocent victim. I'm sure of it."

CHAPTER FOURTEEN

"But didn't he say he had something important to tell you?"

I shook my head. "He said there were things we had to discuss about Steve, but he wasn't specific. I don't think it had anything to do with this."

"It scares me," Debbie said, taking the paper from me and folding it over.

"You're scared because they killed Tommy?" I frowned.

"No — because they did it in front of tens of thousands of people. They must be full of confidence, afraid of nothing. They wouldn't have dared pull a stunt like this a few years ago. They're growing more powerful all the time."

"Overconfidence may prove to be their undoing," I grunted. "They were safer when nobody knew about them. Confidence has brought them out into the light, but they seem to have forgotten — light's no good for creatures of the night."

Debbie put the paper aside. "How's your shoulder?" she asked.

"Not too bad," I said. "But Alice's stitch work leaves a lot to be desired — I'm going to have a terrible scar when the wound heals."

"Another one for the collection," Debbie laughed. Her smile faded. "I noticed a new scar on your back, long and deep. Did you get it when you went away with Harkat?"

I nodded, remembering the monstrous Grotesque, how one of its fangs had caught between my shoulder blades and ripped downwards sharply.

"You still haven't told me what happened, or where you went," Debbie said.

I sighed. "It's not something we need to talk about right now."

"But you found out who Harkat was?"

"Yes," I said, and let the matter drop. I didn't like concealing secrets from Debbie, but if that wasteworld really was the future, I saw no reason to burden Debbie with foreknowledge of it.

I woke early the next morning with a terrible headache. There was a small crack between the curtains, and although only a thin shaft of light was visible, I felt as if a strong torch was being shone directly into my eyes. Groaning, I stumbled out of bed and pulled the curtains closed. That helped, but my headache didn't improve. I lay as still as I could, hoping it would go away. When it didn't, I got out of bed again, meaning to go downstairs and get some aspirin. I passed

Harkat on my way. He was leaning against a wall, asleep, although his lidless eyes were — as always — wide open.

I had taken a few steps down the stairs when a wave of giddiness overcame me and I fell. I grabbed for the banister, managed to catch it before I toppled over, and slid to a bruising halt halfway down the stairs. Head ringing, I sat up and looked around, dazed, wondering if this was an aftereffect of my wounded shoulder. I tried shouting for help but I could only work up a croak.

A short while later, as I lay on the stairs, gathering my strength in an effort to crawl back to my room, Debbie walked by the top of the staircase. She caught site of me and stopped. I raised my head to call her name, but again I could only form a choked croak.

"Declan?" Debbie asked, taking a step forward. "What are you doing? You haven't been drinking again, have you?"

I frowned. Why had she confused me with Declan? We looked nothing alike.

As Debbie climbed down to help, she realized I wasn't the tramp. She stopped, coming on guard. "Who are you?" she snapped. "What are you doing here?"

"It's . . . me," I gasped, but she didn't hear.

"Alice!" Debbie shouted. "Harkat!"

At her cry, Alice and Harkat came running and joined her at the top of the stairs. "Is it one of Declan or Little Kenny's friends?" Alice asked.

"I don't think so," Debbie said.

"Who are you?" Alice challenged me. "Tell us, quick, or —"

"Wait," Harkat interrupted. He stepped past the women and stared hard at me, then grimaced. "As if we haven't enough . . . problems!" He hurried down the steps. "It's OK," he told Alice and Debbie as he picked me up. "It's Darren."

"*Darren?*" Debbie exclaimed. "But he's covered in hair!"

And I realized why she hadn't recognized me. Overnight, my hair had sprouted and I'd grown a beard. "The purge!" I wheezed.

"The second phase." Harkat nodded. "You know what . . . this means?"

Yes — it meant my time as a half-vampire was almost at an end. Within a few weeks the vampire blood within my veins would transform all of the human cells and I'd become a true, night-hugging, sunlight-fearing creature of the dark.

CHAPTER FOURTEEN

I explained the purge to Debbie and Alice. My vampire cells were attacking my human cells, converting them. Within weeks I'd be a full-vampire. In the meantime my body would mature rapidly and undergo all kinds of inconveniences. Apart from the hair, my senses would go haywire. I'd suffer headaches. I'd have to cover my eyes and plug up my nose and ears. My sense of taste would desert me. I'd experience sudden bursts of energy then loss of strength.

"It's terrible timing," I complained to Debbie later in the day. Harkat and Alice were busy elsewhere in the house while Debbie helped me cut my hair and shave.

"What's so bad about it?" she asked.

"I'm vulnerable," I said. "My head's pounding. I can't see, hear, or smell right. I don't know what my body's going to do from one minute to the next. If we get into a fight with the vampaneze anytime soon, I can't be depended upon."

"But you're stronger than normal during the purge, aren't you?"

"Sometimes. But the strength can dwindle away suddenly, leaving me weak and defenseless. And there's no way of predicting when that will happen."

"What about afterwards?" Debbie asked, trimming my fringe. "You'll be a full-vampire?"

"Yes."

"You'll be able to flit and communicate telepathically with other vampires?"

"Not straightaway," I told her. "The ability will be there, but I'll have to develop it. I've got a lot of learning to do over the next few years."

"You don't sound too happy about it," Debbie noted.

I pulled a face. "In many ways I'm glad — I'll finally be a true vampire, as a Prince should be. I've always felt awkward, being a half-vampire and having so much power. On the other hand, I'm facing the end of a way of life. No more sunlight or being able to pass for human. I've enjoyed the best of both worlds since I was blooded. Now I have to leave one of them — the human world — behind forever." I sighed moodily.

Debbie thought about that in silence, cutting my hair back. Then she said quietly, "You'll be an adult at the end, won't you?"

"Yes," I snorted. "That's another change I'm not sure about. I've been a child or a teenager for the better part of thirty years. To leave that behind in the space of a few weeks . . . It's weird!"

"But wonderful," Debbie said. She stopped cutting and stepped in front of me. "Do you remember when you tried to kiss me a few years ago?"

"Yes." I grimaced. "That's when I was pretending to be a student, and you were my teacher. You hit the roof and ordered me out of your apartment."

"Rightly so." Debbie grinned. "As a teacher — an adult — it would be wrong of me to get involved with a child. I couldn't kiss you then, and I can't kiss you now. It'd feel terribly wrong kissing a boy." Her grin changed subtly, mysteriously. "But in a few weeks, you won't be a boy. You'll be a man."

"Oh," I said, thinking about that. Then my expression changed. I gazed up at Debbie with new understanding and hope, then gently took her hand.

CHAPTER FIFTEEN

A BENEFIT OF THE PURGE was that my wound healed quickly and I got my strength back. A couple of days later, I was almost back to full physical fitness, except for my headaches and growing pains.

I was doing push-ups on the floor of my bedroom, working off some of my excess energy, when I heard Debbie squeal downstairs. I stopped instantly and shared a worried look with Harkat, who was standing guard by the door. I hurried to his side and removed one of the earplugs I was wearing to block out the worst of the street noises.

"Should we go down?" Harkat asked, opening the door a crack. We could hear Debbie babbling excitedly, and as we listened, Alice joined her and also began to talk very quickly.

"I don't think anything's wrong," I said, frowning. "They seem happy, as if an old friend has . . ." I stopped and slapped my forehead. Harkat laughed, then both of us said at exactly the same time, "*Vancha!*"

Throwing the door wide open, we barged down the stairs and found Debbie and Alice chatting with a burly red-skinned, green-haired man, dressed in purple animal hides and no shoes, with belts of sharp throwing stars — shurikens — looped around his torso.

"Vancha!" I shouted happily, clutching his arms and squeezing tight.

"It is good to see you again, Sire," Vancha said with surprising politeness. Then he burst into a grin and hugged me tight. "Darren!" he boomed. "I've missed you!" Turning to Harkat, he laughed. "I missed you too, ugly!"

"Look who's talking!" Harkat grinned.

"It's great to see you both, but of course I'm most pleased to see the ladies," Vancha said, releasing me and winking at Debbie and Alice. "Female beauty's what we hot-blooded men live for, aye?"

"He's a born flatterer," Alice sniffed. "I bet he says that to every woman he meets."

"Naturally," Vancha murmured, "because all women are beautiful, in one way or another. But you're more beautiful than most, my dear — an angel of the night!"

Alice snorted with contempt, but there was a strange little smile playing at the corners of her lips. Vancha looped his arms around Debbie and Alice and guided us into the living room, as though this was his house and we were the guests. Sitting down, making himself comfortable, he told Debbie to go fetch some food. She told him — in no uncertain terms — that he could do his own fetching while he was here, and he laughed with delight.

It was refreshing to see that the War of the Scars hadn't changed Vancha March. He was as loud and lively as ever. He filled us in on his recent movements, the countries he'd explored, the vampaneze and vampets he'd killed, making it sound like a big, exciting adventure, free from all consequences.

"When I heard that Leonard was here, I came as quickly as I could," Vancha concluded. "I flitted without rest. I haven't missed him, have I?"

"We don't know," I said. "We haven't heard from him since the night he almost killed me."

"But what does your heart tell you?" Vancha asked, his large eyes weighing heavily upon me, his small mouth closed in a tight expectant line.

"He's here," I said softly. "He's waiting for me — for *us*. I think this is where Mr. Tiny's prophecy will be tested. We'll face him on these streets — or beneath — and we'll kill him or he'll kill us. And that will be the end of the War of the Scars. Except . . ."

"What?" Vancha asked when I didn't continue.

"There was supposed to be one final encounter. Four times our path was due to cross with his. When he had me at his mercy recently, that was the fourth time, but we're both still alive. Maybe Mr. Tiny got it wrong. Maybe his prophecy doesn't hold true any longer."

Vancha mulled that one over. "Perhaps you have a point," he said uncertainly. "But as much as I despise Des Tiny, I have to admit he doesn't make many mistakes when it comes to prophecies — in fact, none that I've heard of. He told you *we* would have four chances to kill Leonard, aye?" I nodded. "Then maybe we both have to be there. Perhaps your solo encounter doesn't count."

"It would have counted if he'd killed me," I grunted.

"But he didn't," Vancha said. "Maybe he couldn't. Perhaps it simply wasn't his destiny."

"If you're right, that means we're going to run into him again," I said.

"Aye," Vancha said. "A fight to the death. Except if he wins, he won't kill both of us. Evanna said one of us would survive if we lost." Evanna was a witch, the daughter of Mr. Tiny. I'd almost forgotten that part of the prophecy. If Steve won, he'd leave one of us alive, to witness the downfall of the clan.

There was a long, troubled silence as we thought about the prophecy and the dangers we faced. Vancha broke it by clapping loudly. "Enough of the doom and gloom! What about you two?" He nodded at Harkat and me. "How did your quest go? Do *we* know who Harkat used to be?"

"Yes," Harkat said. He glanced at Debbie and Alice. "I don't wish to be rude, but could you . . . leave us alone for a while?"

"Is this *men's* talk?" Alice asked mockingly.

"No," Harkat chuckled. "It's *Princes'* talk."

"We'll be upstairs," Debbie said. "Call us when you're ready."

Vancha stood and bowed as the ladies were leaving. When he sat again, his expression was curious. "Why the secrecy?" he asked.

"It's about who I was," Harkat said, "and where . . . we learned the truth. We don't think we should discuss it . . . in front of anybody except a Prince."

"Intriguing," Vancha said, leaning forward eagerly.

We gave Vancha a quick rundown of our quest through the wastelands, the creatures we'd battled, meeting Evanna, the crazy sailor — Spits Abrams — and the dragons. He said nothing, but listened, enthralled. When we told him about pulling Kurda Smahlt out of the Lake of Souls, Vancha's jaw dropped.

"But it can't be!" he protested. "Harkat was alive before Kurda died."

"Mr. Tiny can move through time," I said. "He created Harkat from Kurda's remains, then took him into the past so that he could serve as my protector."

Vancha blinked slowly. Then his features clouded over with rage — and fear. "Damn that Desmond Tiny! I always knew he was powerful, but to be able to meddle with time itself . . . What manner of diabolical beast is he?"

It was a rhetorical question, so we didn't attempt to answer it. Instead we finished by telling him how Kurda had chosen to sacrifice himself — he and Harkat shared a soul, so only one of them could live at any given time — leaving us free to return to the present.

"The *present*?" Vancha snapped. "What do you mean?"

Harkat told him about our theory — that the

wasteworld was the future. When he heard that, Vancha trembled as though a cold wind had sliced through him. "I never thought the War of the Scars could be that crucial," he said softly. "I knew our future was at stake, but I never dreamt we could drag humanity down with us." He shook his head and turned away, muttering, "I need to think about this."

Harkat and I said nothing while Vancha deliberated. Minutes passed. A quarter of an hour. Half an hour. Finally he heaved a large sigh and turned to face us. "These are grim tidings," he said. "But perhaps not as grim as they seem. From what you've told me, I believe that Tiny did take you into the future — but I also believe he wouldn't have done so without good reason. He might have been simply mocking you, but it might also have been a warning.

"That damned future must be what we face if we lose the War of the Scars. Steve Leonard is the sort who'd level the world and bring it to ruin. But if we win, we can prevent that. When Tiny came to Vampire Mountain, he told us there were two possible futures, didn't he? One where the vampaneze win the war, and one where the vampires win. I think Tiny gave you a glimpse of the former future to drive home the point that we *have* to win this war. It's not just ourselves we're fighting for — it's the entire world. The waste-world is one future — I'm sure the world where we've won is completely different."

"It makes sense," Harkat agreed. "If both futures currently exist . . . he might have been able to choose which . . . to take us to."

"Maybe," I sighed, unconvinced. I was thinking again about the vision I'd had shortly after we'd first met Evanna, when Harkat had been plagued by nightmares. Evanna helped me put a stop to them by sending me into his dreams. In the dream, I'd faced a being of immense power — the Lord of the Shadows. Evanna told me this master of evil was part of the future, and the road there was paved with dead souls. She'd also told me that the Lord of the Shadows could be one of two people — Steve Leopard or *me.*

The uncertainties came rushing back. I was unable to share Vancha and Harkat's view that one future was bright and cheery where the other was dark and miserable. I felt we were heading for big-scale trouble, whichever way the War of the Scars swung. But I kept my opinions to myself — I didn't want to come across as a prophet of doom.

"So!" Vancha laughed, startling me out of my dark thoughts. "We just have to make sure we kill Steve Leonard, aye?"

"Aye," I said, grinning sickly.

"What about me?" Harkat asked. "Does it alter your opinion of me . . . now that you know I was once a vampire traitor?"

"No," Vancha said. "I never liked you much anyway." He spat into his right palm, ran the spit through his hair, then winked to show he was joking. "Seriously, you were right not to broadcast the news. We'll keep it to ourselves. I always believed that although Kurda acted stupidly, he acted with the best interests of the clan at heart. But there are many who don't share that view. If they knew the truth about you, it might divide them. Internal argument is the last thing we need. That'd be playing straight into the hands of the vampaneze.

"As for who Harkat is now . . ." Vancha studied the Little Person. "I know you and trust you. I believe you've learned from Kurda's faults. You won't betray us again, will you, Harkat?"

"No," Harkat said softly. "But I'm still in favor of a treaty . . . between the two clans. If I can help bring that about through peaceful . . . means, by talking, I will. This War of the Scars is destroying . . . both families of the night, and it threatens to destroy . . . even more."

"But you recognize the need to fight?" Vancha said sharply.

"I recognize the need to kill Steve . . . Leonard," Harkat said. "After that, I'll push for peace . . . if I can. But openly — no plotting or intrigue . . . this time."

Vancha considered that in silence, then shrugged. "So be it. I have nothing personal against the vampaneze. If we kill Leonard and they agree to a truce, I'm all for it. Now," he continued, scratching his chin, "where do you think Leonard's holed up?"

"Probably somewhere deep underground," I said.

"You think he's preparing a grand-scale trap, like before?" Vancha asked.

"No," Harkat said. "Vampaneze have been active here. That's why Debbie and Alice came. But if there were dozens of them, like . . . the last time, the death count would be higher. I don't think Steve has as many . . . vampaneze with him as when we faced him . . . in the Cavern of Retribution."

"I hope you're right," Vancha said. He glanced at me sideways. "How did my brother look?" Vancha and Gannen Harst were estranged brothers.

"Tired," I said. "Strained. Unhappy."

"Not hard to imagine why," Vancha grunted. "I'll never understand why Gannen and the others follow a maniac like Leonard. The vampaneze were content the way they were. They didn't seek to crush the vampires or provoke a war. It makes no sense for them to flock to that demon and pledge themselves to him."

"It's part of Mr. Tiny's prophecy," Harkat said. "As Kurda, I spent much time with . . . the vampaneze, researching their ways. You know about their Coffin of Fire. When a person lies within, it fills . . . with flames. All normal people die in it. Only the Lord of the Vampaneze . . . can survive. Mr. Tiny told the vampaneze that if they didn't . . . obey that person and do all that he commanded, they'd . . . be wiped from the face of the earth. Most of the vampaneze fight to preserve themselves . . . not to destroy the vampires."

Vancha nodded slowly. "Then they're motivated by fear for their lives, not hatred of us. I understand now. After all, isn't that why we're fighting too — to save ourselves?"

"Both fighting for the same reason," Harkat chuckled humorlessly. "Both terrified of the . . . same thing. Of course, if neither side fought . . . both would be safe. Mr. Tiny is playing the creatures of the night . . . for fools, and we're helping him."

"Aye," Vancha grunted disgustedly. "But there's no use moaning about how we got ourselves into this sorry state. The fact is, we fight because we must."

Vancha stood and stretched. There were dark rims around his eyes. He looked like a man who hadn't slept properly for a very long time. The last two years must have been tough for him. Although he hadn't mentioned Mr. Crepsley, I was sure the dead vampire was never far from his thoughts. Vancha, like I, probably felt a certain amount of guilt — the two of us had give Mr. Crepsley the go-ahead to face the Vampaneze Lord. If either of us had taken his place, he'd be alive now. It looked to me like Vancha had been pushing himself to his limits in his hunt to find the Lord of the Vampaneze — and was rapidly nearing them.

"You should rest, Sire," I said. "If you flitted all the way here, you must be exhausted."

"I'll rest when Leonard is dead," Vancha grunted. "Or myself," he added softly, under his breath. I don't think he realized he'd spoken aloud. "Now!" Vancha said, raising his voice. "Enough self-pity and misery. We're here and Leonard's here — it doesn't take a genius to see that an old-fashioned scrap to the death's on the agenda. The question is, do we wait for him to come to us, or do we seize the initiative and go looking for him?"

"We wouldn't know where . . . to look," Harkat said. "He could be anywhere."

CHAPTER FIFTEEN

"So we look everywhere." Vancha grinned. "But where do we start? Darren?"

"His son," I said immediately. "Darius is an unusual name. There can't be too many of them. We ask around, find out where he lives, track Steve through him."

"Use the son to get to the father," Vancha hummed. "Ignoble, but probably the best way." He paused. "The boy worries me. Leonard's a nasty piece of work, a formidable foe. But if his son has the same evil blood, and has been trained in Leonard's wicked ways since birth, he could be even worse!"

"I agree," I said quietly.

"Can you kill a child, Darren?" Vancha asked.

"I don't know," I said, unable to meet his eyes. "I don't think so. Hopefully it won't come to that."

"It's no good hoping," Harkat objected. "Going after the boy is wrong. Just because Steve has no morals doesn't . . . mean we should act like savages too. Children should be kept out . . . of this."

"So what's your suggestion?" Vancha asked.

"We should return to the . . . Cirque Du Freak," Harkat said. "Hibernius might be able to tell us more . . . about what we should do. Even if he's unable to help, Steve knows . . . where the Cirque is camped. He'll find us there. We can wait for him."

"I don't like the idea of being a sitting target," Vancha growled.

"You'd rather chase children?" Harkat countered.

Vancha stiffened, then relaxed. "Perhaps no-ears has a point," he said. "It can certainly do no harm to ask Hibernius for his opinion."

"OK," I said. "But we'll wait for night — my eyes can't take the sun."

"So that's why your ears and nose are stuffed!" Vancha laughed. "The purge?"

"Yes. It struck a couple of days ago."

"Will you be able to pull your weight," Vancha asked directly, "or should we wait for it to pass?"

"I'll do my best," I said. "I can't make any guarantees, but I think I'll be OK."

"Very well." Vancha nodded at the ceiling. "What about the ladies? Do we tell them what we're up to?"

"Not all of it," I said. "We'll take them to the Cirque Du Freak and tell them we're hunting Steve. But let's not mention Darius — Debbie wouldn't think much of our plan to use a child."

Harkat snorted but said nothing. After that we called Debbie and Alice down and spent a peaceful afternoon eating, drinking and talking, swapping tales, laughing, relaxing. I noticed Vancha glancing around during quiet moments, as though looking for somebody. I dismissed it at the time, but I now know who he was looking for — *death.* Of us all, only Vancha sensed death in the room that day, its eternal gaze passing from one of us to the other, watching . . . waiting . . . choosing.

CHAPTER SIXTEEN

WHEN NIGHT FELL, WE DEPARTED. Declan and Little Kenny bid us farewell. They were settling down in the living room, cell phones laid in front of them like swords. Debbie and Alice's vampirites had been scouring the town for traces of Steve and the other vampaneze since the massacre in the stadium. Declan and Little Kenny were to coordinate that search in the ladies' absence.

"You have our numbers," Alice said to Declan as we were leaving. "Call if you have anything to report, no matter how trivial it might seem."

"Will do." Declan grinned, saluting clumsily.

"Try not to get yourself shot this time," Little Kenny said to me, winking.

Alice and Debbie had a rented van. We piled in, Harkat and Vancha in the back, covered by several blankets. "If we're stopped and searched, you two will have to break free," Alice told them. "We'll act like we didn't know you were there. It'll be easier that way."

"You mean you'll act the innocent and string us out to dry," Vancha grunted.

"Exactly," Alice said.

Even though it was night and the moon was only half-full, I wore sunglasses. My eyes were especially sensitive that night, and I had a splitting headache. I was also wearing earplugs and had little balls of cotton wool stuffed up my nose.

"Maybe you should stay behind," Debbie said, noting my discomfort as Alice switched on the engine.

"I'm OK," I groaned, squinting against the glare of the headlights, wincing at the roaring grumble of the engine.

"We could walk," Alice said, "but we're more likely to be stopped and searched."

"I'm OK," I said again, hunching down in my seat. "Just don't blow the horn."

The drive to the old football stadium where the Cirque Du Freak was encamped was uneventful. We passed two security checkpoints, but were waved through at each. (I took my glasses off and removed the earplugs and cotton wool as we approached, so as not to arouse suspicion.) Alice parked outside the stadium. We let Harkat and Vancha out of the back and walked in.

A big smile broke across my face as the tents and caravans came into sight — it was good to be home. As we exited the tunnel and made for the campsite, we were spotted by a group of children playing on the outskirts. One stood, studied us warily, then raced towards us, yelling, "Godfather! Godfather!"

"Not so loud!" I laughed, catching Shancus as he leapt up to greet me. I gave the snake-boy a welcome hug, then pushed him away — my skin was tingling as a result of the purge, and any form of contact was irritating.

"Why are you wearing sunglasses?" Shancus frowned. "It's night."

"You're so ugly, I can't bear to look at you without protection," I said.

"Very funny," he snorted, then reached up, picked the cotton wool out of my left nostril, examined it, stuck it back in, and said, "You're weird!" He looked behind me at Vancha, Debbie, and Alice. "I remember you guys," he said. "But not very well. I was only a kid the last time I saw you." Smiling, I made the introductions. "Oh yeah," Shancus said when I told him Debbie's name. "You're Darren's girlfriend."

I spluttered with embarrassment and blushed bright red. Debbie just smiled and said, "Am I, indeed? Who told you that?"

"I heard Mom and Dad talking about you. Dad knows you from when you first met Darren. He said Darren goes googly-eyed when you're around. He —"

"That's enough," I interrupted, wishing I could strangle him. "Why don't you show the ladies how you can stick your tongue up your nose?"

That distracted him, and he spent a couple of minutes showing off, telling Alice and Debbie about the act he performed onstage with Evra. I caught Debbie smiling at me sideways. I smiled back weakly.

"Is Truska still with the show?" Vancha asked.

"Yes," Shancus said.

"I must look her up later," Vancha muttered, using a ball of spit to slick back his green hair. The ugly, dirty Prince fancied himself as something of a lady's man — even though no ladies ever agreed with him!

"Is Mr. Tall in his van?" Harkat asked Shancus.

"I guess," Shancus said. Then he glanced at Debbie and Alice and straightened up. "Come with me," he said officiously. "I'll lead you to him."

All five of us fell in behind the snake-boy as he led us through the campsite. He kept up a running commentary, telling Debbie and Alice who the various tents and caravans belonged to, giving them a rundown of that night's coming show. As we neared Mr. Tall's van, we passed Evra, Merla, and Urcha. They had the family snakes out in big tubs of water and were carefully scrubbing them down. Evra was delighted to see me and rushed over to check that I was all right. "I wanted to come visit," he said, "but Hibernius told me it wasn't a good idea. He said I might be followed."

"The Cirque's being watched?" Vancha snapped, eyes narrowing.

"He didn't say so in as many words," Evra said. "But I've felt eyes on my back a few times recently, late at night when I've been wandering around. I'm not the only one. We've all been edgy here lately."

"Maybe we shouldn't have . . . come back," Harkat said, worried.

"Too late now," Vancha huffed. "Let's go see what Hibernius has to say."

Merla grabbed Shancus as he made to lead the way again. "No you don't," she said. "You've a show to prepare for. Don't expect me to groom your snake for you every time you want to go and play with your friends."

"Aw, Mom!" Shancus grumbled, but Merla stuck a sponge in Shancus's hand and dragged him over to the snake I'd bought for his birthday.

"I'll catch up with you later," I laughed, feeling sorry for him. "I'll show you my new scar, where I was shot."

"Another one?" Shancus groaned. He turned appealingly to Evra. "How come Darren gets all the excitement? Why can't *I* get into fights and have scars?"

"Your mother will scar your backside if you don't get busy on that snake," Evra responded, and winked at me over Shancus's head. "Drop by when you have time."

"I will," I promised.

We moved on. Mr. Tall was waiting for us at his van. He was standing in the doorway, looking more impossibly towering than ever, eyes dark, face drawn. "I have been expecting you," he sighed, then stood aside and beckoned us in. As I passed him, a strange shiver ran down my spine. It took me a few seconds to realize what the sensation reminded me of — it was the same sort of feeling I got whenever I saw a dead person.

When we were all seated, Mr. Tall closed the door, then sat on the floor in the middle of us, legs crossed neatly, huge bony hands resting on his knees. "I hope you do not think me rude for not visiting," he said to me. "I knew you would recover, and I had much to put in order here."

"That's OK." I smiled, taking off my sunglasses and putting them to one side.

"It is good to see you again, Vancha," Mr. Tall said, and then welcomed Debbie and Alice.

"Now that the pleasantries are out of the way," Vancha grunted, "let's get down to business. You knew what was going to happen at the football arena, aye?"

"I had my suspicions," Mr. Tall said cagily, his lips barely moving.

"But you let Darren go regardless? You let his friend die?"

"I did not 'let' anything happen," Mr. Tall disagreed. "Events unfolded the way they had to. It is not my place to interfere in the unraveling of destiny. You know that, Vancha. We have had this conversation before. Several times."

"And I still don't buy it," Vancha grumbled. "If *I* had the power to see into the future, I'd use it to help those I cared about. You could have told us who the Lord of the Vampaneze was. Larten would be alive now if you'd warned us."

"No," Mr. Tall said. "Larten would have died. The circumstances might have differed, but his death was inevitable. I could not have altered that."

"You should still have tried," Vancha persisted.

Mr. Tall smiled thinly, then looked at me. "You have come to seek guidance. You wish to know where your one-time friend, Steve Leonard, is."

"Can you tell us?" I asked softly.

"No," Mr. Tall said. "But rest assured, he will make himself known soon. You will not have to dredge the depths for him."

"Does that mean he's going to attack?" Vancha pressed. "Is he nearby? When does he plan to strike? Where?"

"I grow weary of your questions," Mr. Tall growled, his eyes flashing menacingly. "If I could step in and play an active part in the affairs of the vampire clan, I would. It is much harder to stand back and watch passively. Harder than you could ever imagine. You wept for Larten when he died — but *I* grieved for him for thirty years in advance, since glimpsing his probable death."

"You mean you didn't know for . . . sure that he'd die?" Harkat asked.

"I knew he would come to the point where it was his life or the Lord of the Vampaneze's, but I could not see beyond that — though I feared the worst."

CHAPTER SIXTEEN

"And what of our next encounter?" I asked quietly. "When Vancha and I face Steve for the last time — who'll die then?"

"I do not know," Mr. Tall said. "Looking into the future is more often than not a painful experience. It is better not to know the fate of your friends and loved ones. I lift the lid off the present as seldom as possible. There are times when I cannot avoid it, when my own destiny forces me to look. But only rarely."

"So you don't know if we'll win or lose?" I asked.

"Nobody knows that," Mr. Tall said. "Not even Desmond Tiny."

"But *if* we lose," I said, and there was an edge to my voice now. "If the vampaneze are triumphant, and Steve kills one of us — which will it be?"

"I don't know," Mr. Tall said.

"But you could find out," I pressed. "You could look into the future where we've lost and see which of us survived."

"Why should I?" Mr. Tall sighed. "What profit would there be in it?"

"I want to know," I insisted.

"Maybe it would be better —" Vancha began to say.

"No!" I hissed. "I *must* know. For two years I've dreamt of the destruction of the clan, and listened to the screams of those who'll perish if we fail. If I'm to die, so be it. But tell me, please, so I can prepare myself for it."

"I cannot," Mr. Tall said unhappily. "Nobody can predict which of you will kill the Vampaneze Lord — or die at his hand."

"Then look further ahead," I pleaded. "Go twenty years ahead, or thirty. Do you see Vancha or me in that future?"

"Leave me out of this!" Vancha snapped. "I don't want to mess about with stuff like that."

"Then just look for me," I said, staring hard at Mr. Tall.

Mr. Tall held my gaze, then said quietly, "You are sure?"

I stiffened. "Yes!"

"Very well." Mr. Tall lowered his gaze and closed his eyes. "I cannot be as specific as you state, but I will cast my eyes a number of decades forward and . . ."

Mr. Tall trailed off into silence. Vancha, Harkat, Debbie, Alice, and I watched, awed, as his face twitched and glowed a light red color. The owner of the Cirque Du Freak seemed to stop breathing and the temperature of the air dropped several degrees. For five minutes he held that pose, face glowing and twitching, lips sealed. Then he breathed out, the glow faded, his eyes opened, and the temperature returned to normal.

CHAPTER SIXTEEN

"I have looked," he said, his expression unreadable.

"And?" I croaked.

"I did not find you there."

I smiled bitterly. "I knew it. If the clan falls, it will fall because of *me*. I'm the doomed one in the future where we lose."

"Not necessarily," Mr. Tall said. "I looked fifty or sixty years ahead, long after the fall of the vampires. You might have died after all of the others had been killed."

"Then bring it forward," I demanded. "Look twenty or thirty years ahead."

"No," Mr. Tall said stiffly. "I have already seen more than I wished. I don't want to suffer any further tonight."

"What are you talking about?" I huffed. "What have you suffered?"

"Grief," Mr. Tall said. He paused, then glanced at Vancha. "I know you told me not to look for you, old friend, but I couldn't help myself."

Vancha cursed, then braced himself. "Go on. Since this fool's opened the can of worms, we might as well watch them wriggle. Hit me with the bad news."

"I looked into both futures," Mr. Tall said hollowly. "I did not mean to, but I cannot control these things. I looked into the future where the vampaneze won the War of the Scars, and also into the future where the vampires won — and although I found Darren in the latter future, I found you in neither." He locked gazes with Vancha and muttered gloomily, "You were killed by the Lord of the Shadows in both."

CHAPTER SEVENTEEN

VANCHA BLINKED SLOWLY. "You're saying I'll die whether we win or lose?" His voice was surprisingly steady.

"The Lord of the Shadows is destined to destroy you," Mr. Tall replied. "I cannot say when or how it happens, but it will."

"Who's this Lord of the Shadows?" Harkat asked. I was the only person who'd been told about him. Evanna had warned me not to speak of it to anybody else.

"He's the cruel leader who will ruin the world after the War of the Scars," Mr. Tall said.

"I don't get it," Harkat grumbled. "If we kill Steve, then there won't be a . . . Lord of the bloody Shadows."

"Oh, but there will," Mr. Tall said. "The world is set to produce a monster of unimaginable power and fury. His coming is unavoidable. Only his identity is yet to be determined — and that will be decided shortly."

"The wasteworld," Harkat said sickly. "You mean, even if we kill Steve, that's what . . . the future will be? The desolate land where Darren and I found . . . out the truth about me — that's what lies . . . in store?"

Mr. Tall hesitated, then nodded. "I could not tell you before. I have never spoken of matters such as this in the past. But we are at the time where no harm can come of revealing it, since nothing can be done to avert it. The Lord of the Shadows is upon us — within twenty-four hours he will be born, and all the world will tremble at his coming."

There was a long, stunned silence. Vancha, Harkat, Debbie, and Alice were filled with confusion, especially the latter pair, who knew nothing of the wasteworld of the future. *I* was filled with fear. This was confirmation of all my worst nightmares. The Lord of the Shadows would rise regardless of what happened in the War of the Scars. And not only could I not prevent his coming — in one of the futures, I would *be* him. Which meant, if we won the war, at some stage in the next fifty or sixty years, along with all the other lives I'd ruin, I would kill Vancha too. It seemed impossible. It sounded like a sick joke. But Evanna and Mr. Tall both had the gift of reading the future — and both had told me the same thing.

"Let me get this straight," Vancha growled, breaking the silence and disrupting my train of thought. "No matter what happens between us and Steve Leonard — or in the war with the vampaneze — a Lord of the Shadows is going to come along and destroy the world?"

"Yes," Mr. Tall said. "Humans are soon to lose control of this planet. The reins of power will be handed over. This is written. What remains to be seen is whether the reins pass to a vampaneze or . . . to a vampire." He didn't look at me when he said that. It might have been my imagination, but I got the feeling he had deliberately avoided making eye contact with me.

"But regardless of who wins, I'm for the chop?" Vancha pressed.

"Yes." Mr. Tall smiled. "But do not fear death, Vancha, for it comes for us all." His smile dimmed. "For some of us, it comes very soon."

"What are you talking about?" Vancha snapped. "You're not part of this. No vampire or vampaneze would raise a hand against you."

"That might be true," Mr. Tall chuckled, "but there are others in this world who do not hold me in such high esteem." He cocked his head sideways and his expression mellowed. "And to prove my point . . ."

A woman screamed. We all sprang to our feet and rushed to the door, except Mr. Tall, who slowly rose behind us.

Alice was the first to the door. Flinging it open, she dived out, drew a gun, rolled when she hit the ground, then came to her knees. Vancha was next. He leapt out, pulling a couple of shurikens free, jumping high to launch them from a height if he had to. I was third. I had no weapons, so I sprang over to where Alice was, guessing she'd be able to supply me with something. Harkat and Debbie moved at the same time, Harkat brandishing his axe, Debbie pulling a pistol like Alice's. Behind them, Mr. Tall stood in the doorway, gazing up at the sky. Then he stepped down.

There was nobody in sight, but we heard another scream, this time a child's. Then a man gave a shout of panic — it was Evra.

"A weapon!" I yelled at Alice as she got to her feet. With one hand she reached down and produced a short hunting knife from a pouch on her left leg.

"Stay behind me," Alice commanded, homing in on the screams. "Vancha to my left, Debbie and Harkat to my right."

CHAPTER SEVENTEEN

We obeyed the ex–chief inspector, fanned out, and advanced. I could sense Mr. Tall following, but I didn't look back.

A woman screamed again — Merla, Evra's wife.

People spilled out of the caravans and tents around us, performers and staff, eager to help. Mr. Tall roared at them to keep out of this. His voice was thunderous and they quickly bolted back inside. I glanced over my shoulder, stunned by his fierceness. He smiled apologetically. "This is our fight, not theirs," he said by way of explanation.

The "our" surprised me — was Mr. Tall finally abandoning his neutrality? — but I didn't have time to dwell upon it. Ahead of me, Alice had cleared the end of a tent and come into sight of the disturbance. A second later, I was on the scene too.

The Vons — except Lilia, who wasn't present — were under attack. Their assailants — R.V., Morgan James, and Steve Leopard's son, Darius! R.V. had killed Evra's snake and was in the process of chopping up Shancus's. Evra was fighting with the hook-handed madman, trying to drag him off. Shancus was in a wrestling lock with Darius. Merla had hold of Urcha, who was gripping his snake for dear life, sobbing pitifully. They were backing away from Morgan James. He was following slowly, smiling a jagged half-faced smile, red circles of blood highlighting his evil little eyes. The nose of his rifle was aimed at Merla's stomach.

Vancha reacted quickest. He sent a shuriken flying at Morgan James's rifle, knocking it off target. James's finger tightened on the trigger at the contact and the rifle exploded — but the bullet shot wide. Before he could fire again, Merla released Urcha, ripped her right ear loose, and sent it flying at James's face. The ear struck him between the eyes and he fell back, grunting with surprise.

Alerted to our presence, R.V. knocked Evra out of the way and dove after Shancus. He grabbed him from Darius and held him up, laughing, daring us to risk the snake-boy's life.

"I don't have a clear shot!" Alice yelled.

"I've got Morgan James covered!" Debbie shouted back.

"Then take him out!" Alice roared.

"The boy dies if you hurt Morgan!" R.V. retorted, pressing the three blades of his hooked left hand up into the scaly flesh of Shancus's throat. Shancus either didn't realize the danger he was in, or didn't care, because he kept kicking and punching R.V. But we saw the killer's intent and paused.

CHAPTER SEVENTEEN

"Let him go, Hooky," Vancha snarled, moving ahead of the rest of us, hands spread wide. "I'll fight you man to man."

"You're no man," R.V. replied scornfully. "You're scum like all your race. Morgan! Are you OK?"

"Uh'm fuhn," Morgan James groaned. He picked up his rifle and aimed it at Merla again.

"Not this time!" Harkat shouted, stepping in front of Merla and swinging at James with his axe. James leapt clear of the deadly blade. Across from him, Darius drew a small arrow-gun and fired at Harkat. But he fired too hastily and the arrow flew high of its mark.

I threw myself at Darius, meaning to grab and hold him, as R.V. was holding Shancus. But Shancus's snake was thrashing wildly in its death throes, and I tripped over it before I could bring my hands together around Darius's throat. Flying forward, I crashed into Evra, who was rushing to his son's aid. We both fell over, wrapped in the dying snake's coils.

During the confusion, Morgan James and Darius regrouped around R.V.

Alice, Debbie, Harkat, and Vancha hung back, unable to pursue them for fear that R.V. would kill Shancus.

"Let him go!" Merla screamed, eyes filled with tears of desperation.

"Make me!" R.V. jeered.

"You can't get out of here," Vancha said as R.V. backed away.

"Who's going to stop us?" R.V. mocked him.

Evra was back on his feet and he made to run after the retreating trio. R.V. dug his hooks deeper into Shancus's throat. "No you don't!" he sang, and Evra froze.

"Please," Debbie said, lowering her pistol. "Release the boy and we'll let you leave unharmed."

"You're in no position to make deals," R.V. laughed.

"What do you want?" I shouted.

"The snake-boy," R.V. giggled.

"He's no good to you." I took a determined step forward. "Take me instead. I'll swap for Shancus."

I expected R.V. to leap at my offer, but he only shook his head slyly, red eyes shining. "Stuff it, Shan," he said. "We're taking the boy. If you get in our way, he dies."

I glanced around at my allies — nobody was reacting. The vampaneze had us in a bind. Vancha could move with the speed of a full-vampire, and Debbie and

Alice both had guns. But R.V. could kill Shancus before any of us could stop him.

R.V., Morgan James, and Darius continued to back away. R.V. and James were grinning, but Darius looked the same way he'd looked after shooting me — scared and slightly sickened.

Then, as the rest of us hesitated, Mr. Tall spoke. "I cannot allow this."

R.V. paused uncertainly. "This is none of your business!" he shouted. "Keep your nose out of it."

"You have made it my business," Mr. Tall disagreed quietly. "This is my home. These are my people. I must intervene."

"Don't be a —" R.V. yelled, but before he got any further, Mr. Tall was upon him. He moved at a supernatural speed that even a vampire couldn't match. In less than a flash of an eye he was in front of R.V., his hands on the lunatic's hooks. He wrenched them away from Shancus's throat, tearing two of the hooks off the left hand, and one off the right.

"My hands!" R.V. screamed in agony, as though the gold and silver hooks were part of his flesh. "Leave my hands alone, you —"

Whatever foul name he shouted was lost in the burst of a gun retort. Morgan James, who'd been standing next to R.V., had jammed the tip of his rifle hard into Mr. Tall's ribs and pulled the trigger. A bullet fired down the chamber of the rifle at a merciless speed — then ripped through the rib cage of the defenseless Hibernius Tall!

CHAPTER EIGHTEEN

MR. TALL'S MIDRIFF ERUPTED in a fountain of dark red blood and white chips of bone. For a moment he stood, gripping R.V.'s hooks, as though nothing had happened. Then he collapsed, blood pumping out of the hole, his stomach torn to shreds.

R.V. and Darius stared numbly at Mr. Tall as he fell. Then Morgan James screamed at them to run. In a ragged unit they fled, R.V. clutching Shancus, James firing wildly at us over his shoulder.

Nobody followed. Our eyes were all on Mr. Tall. He was blinking rapidly, hands exploring the hole in his middle, lips torn back over his small black teeth. I don't think anybody knew how old Mr. Tall was, or where he'd come from. But he was older than any vampire, a being of immense magic and power. It was mind-boggling to think that he could have been brought low in so simple and violent a manner.

Debbie snapped to her senses first and rushed towards Mr. Tall, dropping her pistol, meaning to go to his aid. The rest of us took a step after her —

— and stopped instantly when somebody spoke from the shadows of a nearby van. "Your concern is commendable, but utterly worthless. Keep back, please."

A small man waddled forward, smiling glibly. He was dressed in a sharp yellow suit and green rain boots. He had white hair, thick glasses, and a heart-shaped watch that he was twirling in his left hand. *Desmond Tiny!* Behind him came his daughter, the witch Evanna — short, muscular, hairy, clad in ropes instead of clothes. She had a small nose, pointed ears, a thin beard, and mismatched eyes, one brown, one green.

We gaped at the strange pair as they stopped beside the gasping Mr. Tall and gazed down at him. Evanna's face was strained. Mr. Tiny looked only curious. With his right foot, he nudged Mr. Tall where he'd been shot. Mr. Tall hissed with pain.

"Leave him alone!" Debbie shouted.

"Shut up, please, or I'll kill you," Mr. Tiny replied. Though he said it sweetly, I've no doubt he would have struck Debbie down dead if she'd said another word. Fortunately, she realized that too, and she held her tongue, trembling.

"So, Hibernius," Mr. Tiny said. "Your time here comes to an end."

"You knew it would," Mr. Tall replied, and his voice was remarkably firm.

"Yes." Mr. Tiny nodded. "But did *you* know?"

"I guessed."

"You could have turned aside from it. Your fate was never directly linked to these mortals."

"For me, it was," Mr. Tall said. He was shivering badly, a dark pool of blood spreading out around him. Evanna took a step aside to avoid the blood, but Mr. Tiny let it flow around his boots, staining the soles.

"Tiny!" Vancha snapped. "Can you save him?"

"No," Mr. Tiny replied simply. Then he bent over Mr. Tall and spread the fingers of his right hand. He placed his middle finger in the center of Mr. Tall's forehead, the adjoining fingers over his eyes, and held the thumb and little finger out at the sides. "Even in death, may you be triumphant," he said with surprising softness, then removed his fingers.

"Thank you, father," Mr. Tall said. He glanced up at Evanna. "Goodbye, sister."

"I will remember you," the witch answered as the rest of us looked on, stunned by the revelation. I'd known about Evanna's twin brother, born, as she was, of a union between Mr. Tiny and a wolf. I'd just never guessed it was Mr. Tall.

Evanna bent and kissed her brother's forehead. Mr. Tall smiled, then his body shook, his eyes went wide, his neck stiffened — and he died.

Mr. Tiny stood and turned. There was one round tear of blood in the corner of each eye. "My son is dead," he said, in the same tone he'd have used to comment on the weather.

"We didn't know!" Vancha gasped.

"He never cared to speak of his parentage." Mr. Tiny chuckled and kicked the dead Mr. Tall's head aside with the heel of his left foot. "I don't know why."

I growled when he kicked Mr. Tall, and started towards him angrily. Harkat and Vancha did the same.

"Gentlemen," Evanna said quietly. "If you waste time picking a fight with my father, the killers will escape with the young Von boy."

We stopped short. I'd momentarily forgotten about Shancus and the danger he was in. The others had too. Now that we'd been reminded, we shook our heads and snapped out of our daze.

"We have to chase them," Vancha said.

"But what about Mr. Tall?" Debbie cried.

"He's dead," Vancha sniffed. "Let his *family* care for him."

Mr. Tiny laughed at that, but we couldn't afford to pay him any further heed. Grouping together without discussing it, the five of us set off. "Wait!" Evra shouted. I looked back and saw him exchange a wordless look with Merla. She half-nodded and he ran after us. "I'm coming too," he said.

Nobody argued. Accepting Evra into our ranks, we raced away from Merla, Urcha, Mr. Tiny, Evanna, and the dead Mr. Tall, and hurried through the campsite in pursuit of Shancus and his kidnappers.

As soon as we cleared the tunnel leading out of the stadium, we saw that our quarry had split. To our right, R.V. was running away with Shancus, headed into the heart of town. To our left, Morgan James and Darius fled down the hill towards a river that flowed close by the stadium.

Vancha took charge and made a swift decision. "Alice and Evra — with me. We'll go after R.V. and Shancus. Darren, Harkat, and Debbie — take Morgan James and the boy."

I'd rather have gone to Shancus's rescue, but Vancha was more experienced than me. Nodding obediently, I swung left with Harkat and Debbie and we set off after the killer and his apprentice. My headache had flared up savagely and I was half-blind as I flailed down the hill. Also, the sounds of my feet on the pavement as I ran were torture on my ears. Still, as a half-vampire I could run faster than Harkat or Debbie, and I'd soon pulled ahead and was rapidly closing the gap on Morgan James and Darius.

James and Darius stopped when they heard me coming and spun to face my charge. I should have waited for Harkat and Debbie, rather than face them on my own, armed only with a knife. But rage had taken hold of me. I forged on heedlessly as they fired, James with his rifle, Darius with his arrow-gun. By the luck of the vampires, their bullets and arrows missed, and seconds later I was upon them, wild with fury, intent on revenge.

James swung at me with the butt of his rifle. It struck my right shoulder, where I'd been shot by Darius. I roared with pain but didn't falter. I stabbed at James with my knife, aiming for his half-mangled face. He ducked, and Darius punched me in the ribs as I slid past. I swatted the boy aside and stabbed at James again. He laughed and grabbed me tight, wrestling me to the ground.

My face was pressed up close to the left side of Morgan James's head. The skin was wrinkled and red, his teeth exposed behind the thin flesh of his lips, his eye a horrible glob in the middle of a ruined, scarred mess.

"Lyhk iht?" James gurgled.

"Lovely!" I sneered, rolling on top of him, poking for his eyes with my thumbs.

"Uh'm gonna duh the shahm tuh yuh!" James vowed, breaking my grip and driving his knee up into my stomach.

"We'll see!" I grunted, falling away slightly, then coming back at him. I managed to stick my knife in, but only into his arm. I was aware of the boy battering me with his arrow-gun, trying to beat me off. I ignored him and focused on Morgan James. I was stronger than the vampet, but he was larger and a seasoned fighter. He wriggled beneath me, digging his knees and elbows into the flesh of my stomach and groin, spitting into my eyes. There was a painful white light building inside my head. I felt like screaming and clapping my hands over my ears. But instead I bit into the flesh of James's upper left arm and ripped a chunk away.

James screeched like a cat and shoved me off, lent

strength by his pain. As I fell aside, Darius kicked me hard in the head and I lost my bearings for a second or two. When I recovered, James was on top of me. He pushed my head back with his left hand and brought up my own knife — which I'd dropped in the fight — with his right, meaning to slit my throat.

I grabbed for the knife. Missed. Grabbed again. Knocked it aside. Grabbed a third time — then stopped, tensed my muscles, and shut my eyes. James gave a little shiver of delight. He thought I'd given up. What he didn't realize was that I'd caught sight of Harkat behind him, swinging his axe.

There was a whishing sound — Darius started to shout a warning — then a heavy thud. My eyes opened. I caught a glimpse of Morgan James's head rolling away into darkness, severed from its body by one powerful blow of Harkat's axe. Then blood gushed from the stump of James's neck. I shut my eyes again as I was drenched in a burst of hot red liquid. James fell over lifelessly. I pushed myself up, opened my eyes, wiped blood from my face, and slid out from beneath the beheaded body of Morgan James.

Darius was standing next to me, staring numbly at his felled companion. Blood had hit the boy also, drenching his pants. I stood. My legs were trembling. My head was filled with white noise. Blood congealed in my hair and dripped from my face. I wanted to be sick. But I knew what I must do. Hatred motivated me.

Snatching my knife from Morgan James's lifeless hand, I pressed the blade to the flesh of Darius's throat and grabbed his hair with my free hand. I was snarling as I pressed down hard on the knife, neither human nor vampire. I'd become a savage animal set on taking a young boy's life.

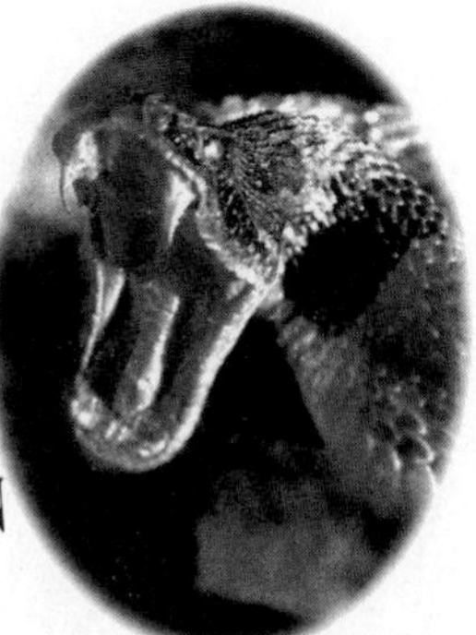

CHAPTER NINETEEN

DEBBIE STOPPED ME. *"No!"* she screamed, racing up behind me. There was such terror in her voice that even in the midst of my bloodlust, I paused. She pulled up beside me, panting hard, eyes wide with horror. "No!" she wheezed, shaking her head desperately.

"Why not?" I snarled.

"He's a child!" she cried.

"No — he's Steve Leopard's son," I contradicted her. "A killer, like his father."

"He hasn't killed anyone," Debbie objected. "Morgan James killed Mr. Tall. Now he's dead, you're even. You don't have to kill the boy too."

"I'll kill them all!" I screamed madly. It was like I'd become a different person, a bloodthirsty reaper. "Every vampaneze must die! Every vampet! Everyone who aids them!"

"Even the children?" Debbie asked sickly.

"Yes!" I roared. My headache was the worst it had ever been. It was like red-hot pins were being pushed through my skull from the inside out. Part of me knew this was wrong, but a larger part had seized on the hatred and urge to kill. That merciless part was screaming for revenge.

"Harkat," Debbie appealed to the Little Person. "Make him see sense!"

Harkat shook his neckless head. "I don't think I can stop him," he said, staring at me as if he didn't know me.

"You have to try!" Debbie shrieked.

"I don't know if I . . . have the right," Harkat muttered.

Debbie turned to me again. She was crying. "You mustn't do this," she wept.

"It's my duty," I said stiffly.

She spat at my feet. "That's what I think of your *duty*! You'll become a monster if you kill that boy. You'll be no better than Steve."

I stopped. Her words had sparked a memory deep within me. I found myself thinking about Mr. Crepsley and his last words to me before he died. He warned me not to devote my life to hatred. Kill Steve Leopard if the chance presented itself — but don't give myself over to some insane revenge quest.

What would he have done in my place? Kill the boy? Yes, if necessary. But *was* it? Did I want to kill Darius because I feared him and felt he had to be eliminated for the good of us all — or because I wanted to hurt Steve?

I gazed into the boy's eyes. They were fearful, but behind the fear there was . . . sorrow. In Steve's eyes, evil lurked deep down. Not in Darius. He was more human than his father.

My knife was still pressed to his throat. It had sliced thinly into his flesh. Little rivulets of blood trickled down his neck.

"You'll destroy yourself," Debbie whispered hoarsely. "You'll be worse than Steve. *He* can't tell the difference between right and wrong. *You* can. He can live with his wickedness because he doesn't know any better, but it will eat you away. Don't do it, Darren. We don't wage war on children."

I stared at her, tears in my eyes. I knew she was right. I wanted to take the knife away. I couldn't believe I'd even tried to kill the boy. But still there was part of me that wanted to take his life. Something had awoken within me, a Darren Shan I'd never known existed, and he wasn't going to lie down without a fight. My fingers shook as they held the knife, but the furious angel of revenge inside me wouldn't let me lower them.

"Go ahead and kill me," Darius snarled suddenly. "It's what your kind does. You're murderers. I know all about you, so stop pretending you give a damn."

"What are you talking about?" I said. He only smiled sickly in reply.

"He's Steve's son," Debbie said softly. "He's been raised on lies. That's not his fault."

"My father doesn't lie!" Darius shouted.

Debbie moved around behind Darius so she could look me straight in the eye. "He doesn't know the truth. He's innocent, in spite of anything he's been tricked into doing. Don't kill an innocent, Darren. Don't become what you despise."

I groaned deeply. More than ever I wanted to take the knife away, but still I wavered, fighting an inner battle that I didn't completely understand. "I don't know what to do!" I moaned.

"Then think of this," Harkat said. "We might need the boy to swap . . . for Shancus. It makes sense not to kill him."

The fire within me died away. I lowered my knife, feeling a great weight lift from my heart. I smiled crookedly. "Thanks, Harkat."

CHAPTER NINETEEN

"You shouldn't have needed that," Debbie said as I spun Darius around and tied his hands behind him with a strip of cloth that Harkat had ripped from his robes. "You should have spared him because it was the right thing to do — not because you might need him."

"Maybe," I agreed, ashamed of my reaction but not wanting to admit it. "But it doesn't matter. We can debate it later. First, let's find out what's happening with Shancus. Where's your phone?"

A minute later she was deep in conversation with Alice Burgess. They were still in pursuit of R.V. and Shancus. Vancha asked to speak to me. "We have a choice to make," he said. "I have R.V. in my sights. I can cut him down with a shuriken and rescue Shancus."

"Then why don't you?" I frowned.

"I think he's leading us to Steve Leonard," Vancha said.

I groaned softly and gripped the phone tightly. "What does Evra say?" I asked.

"This is our call, not his," Vancha responded with a whisper. "He's thinking only of his son. We have other concerns to consider."

"I'm not prepared to sacrifice Shancus to get to Steve," I said.

"I am," Vancha said quietly. "But I doubt it will come to that. I think we can retrieve the boy *and* get a shot at Leonard. But it's a risk. If you want me to play it safe and kill R.V. now, I will. But I believe we should chance it, let him lead us to Leonard, and take it from there."

"You're the senior Prince," I said. "You decide."

"No," Vancha retorted. "We're equals. Shancus means more to you than he does to me. I'll follow your lead on this one."

"Thanks," I said bitterly.

"Sorry," Vancha said, and even over the phone I could tell his regret was genuine. "I'd take responsibility if I could, but on this occasion I can't. Do I kill R.V. or follow?"

My eyes flicked to Darius. If I'd killed him, I'd have told Vancha to bring R.V. down and save Shancus — otherwise Steve would surely slaughter the snake-boy in revenge. But if I turned up with Darius captive, Steve would have to trade. Once we had Shancus back, we'd be free to pursue Steve later.

"OK," I said. "Let him run. Tell me where you are and we'll catch up."

A few minutes later we were on the move again, cutting across town, Debbie on the phone to Alice, taking directions. I could feel her eyes burning into my back — she didn't approve of the risk we were taking — but I didn't look around. As I ran, I kept reminding myself, "I'm a Prince. I have a duty to my people. The Lord of the Vampaneze takes priority over all." But it was a slim comfort, and I knew my sense of guilt and shame would be overwhelming if the gamble backfired.

CHAPTER TWENTY

WE WERE HURRYING through the streets with Darius, taking back alleys to avoid the police patrols, when Harkat slowed, came to a stop, and turned. He cocked his head sideways, raising one of the ears stitched beneath his grey skin.

"What is it?" I asked.

"Footsteps . . . behind us. Can't you hear?"

"My ears are plugged up," I reminded him. "Are you certain?"

"Yes. I think it's just one person, but I . . . could be wrong."

"We can't fight and hold on to Darius at the same time," Debbie said. "If we're to make a stand, we should either tie him up or let him go."

"I'm not letting him go anywhere," I muttered. "You two proceed. If R.V. leads the others to Steve, you need to be there with Darius, to trade for Shancus. I'll stay and deal with this. If I can, I'll catch up."

"Don't be stupid," Debbie hissed. "We've got to stick together."

"Do what I say!" I snapped, harsher than necessary. I was very confused — hatred for Steve, fear that I might become the monstrous Lord of the Shadows, the pain of the purge — and in no mood to argue.

"Come on," Harkat said to Debbie. "We can't talk to him when he's . . . like this. Besides, he's right. It makes more sense this way."

"But the danger —" Debbie began.

"He's a Vampire Prince," Harkat said. "He knows all about danger."

Harkat jerked Darius ahead, limping forward as quickly as he could. Debbie had no choice but to follow, though she looked back imploringly at me before turning a corner out of sight. I felt sorry for the way I'd snapped at her, and hoped I'd have a chance to apologize later.

I removed the cotton buds from my ears and nose and took a firm grip on my knife. By concentrating hard, I could dim the noise within my head and focus on the street sounds and scents. I heard footsteps approaching, soft, steady, coming straight towards me. I crouched low and readied myself for battle. Then a figure came into sight and I relaxed, stood, and lowered my knife arm.

"Evanna," I greeted the witch.

"Darren," she replied calmly, stopping close by, studying me with an unreadable expression.

"Why aren't you with your father?" I asked.

"I will join him again presently," she said. "My place is here now, with you and your allies. Let us hurry after them, for fear we miss the confrontation."

"I'm going nowhere," I said, standing my ground. "Not until you give me some answers."

"Indeed?" Evanna purred archly. "I will need to hear some questions first."

"It's about the Lord of the Shadows."

"I don't think this is the time —"

"I don't care what you think!" I interrupted. "You told me years ago that the Lord of the Shadows would be either the Vampaneze Lord — Steve — or *me*. Mr. Tall, before he died, said that the Lord of the Shadows would rise no matter who won the War of the Scars."

"Did he?" Evanna sounded surprised. "It was not like Hibernius to be so revealing. He was always the more secretive one."

"I want to know what it means," I pressed on, before she got sidetracked talking about her dead brother.

"According to Mr. Tall, the Lord of the Shadows will be a monster, and he'll kill Vancha."

"He told you that too?" Evanna was angry now. "He went too far. He should not have —"

"But he did," I stopped her, then took a step nearer. "He was wrong. He must have been. You too. I'm no monster. I would never harm Vancha, or any vampire."

"Don't be too sure of that," she said softly, then hesitated, choosing her next words carefully. "Usually there are many paths between the present and future, dozens of options and outcomes. But sometimes there are only a few, or even just two. That is the case here. A Lord of the Shadows will come — this is definite. But he can be one of two people, you or Steve Leonard."

"But —" I began.

"Silence," she said commandingly. "Since we are so close to the time of choosing, I can reveal certain facts that before I could not. I wouldn't have spoken of this, but it seems my brother wished to inform you of your fate, perhaps to give you time to prepare for it. It is only right that I honor his final wishes.

"If you kill Steve Leonard, you *will* become a monster, the most despised and twisted the world has ever seen." My eyes bulged and I opened my mouth to protest, but she continued before I uttered a syllable.

"Monsters are not born fully developed. They grow, they mature, they *become*.

"You are filling with hatred, Darren, hatred that will consume you. If you kill Steve, it will not be enough. You'll push on, driven by rages you cannot control. Because destiny has marked you out as a bearer of great power, you will create great havoc. You will destroy the vampaneze but that won't be enough. There will always be a new enemy to fight. During your quest, certain vampires will try to stop you. They too will die at your hands. Vancha will be one of them."

"No," I moaned. "I would never —"

"Not only vampires will obstruct you," Evanna went on, ignoring my protests. "Humans will interfere, leading you to turn against them. And, as the vampaneze and vampires fall at your hands, so will humanity. You will reduce this world to rubble and ash. And over the remains you will rule, all-powerful, all-controlling, all-hating, for the rest of your unnaturally long and evil life."

She stopped and smiled at me witheringly. "That is your future, where you taste success. In the other, you die at the hands of the alternate Lord of the Shadows, if not during the hunt for him, then later, when the rest of the clan has fallen. In many ways, that might be for the best. Now, any more questions?"

"I couldn't," I said numbly. "I wouldn't. There must be some way to avoid it."

"There is," Evanna said. She turned and pointed back the way she'd come. "Go. Walk away. Leave your friends. Hide. If you go now, you'll break the terms of your destiny. Steve will lead the vampaneze to victory over the vampires and become the Lord of the Shadows. You can lead a normal, peaceful life — until he brings the world crashing down around you, of course."

"But . . . I can't do that," I said. "I can't turn my back on those who've put their trust in me. What about Vancha, Debbie, Shancus? I have to help them."

"Yes," Evanna said sadly. "I know. That is why you cannot escape. You have the power to run from your destiny, but your feelings for your friends won't allow you. You'll never retreat from a challenge. You can't. And so, even though you have the best will in the world, you'll see your destiny through to its bitter end — either death by Steve's hand, or a rise to infamy as the Lord of the Shadows."

"You're wrong," I said shakily. "I won't do that. I'm not evil. Now that I know, I won't let myself go down that road. If I kill Steve . . . if we win . . . I'll turn my back on my destiny then. I'll save the clan if I can, then slip away. I'll go where I can't do any harm."

CHAPTER TWENTY

"No," Evanna said simply. "You won't. Now," she went on before I could argue my case again, "let us hurry after your friends — this night is central to the future, and it would not do to miss a moment more of it." With that, she slid ahead of me and followed after the others, tracking them by means of her own, leaving me to trail behind, silent, dejected, bewildered — and terrified.

We caught up with Debbie, Harkat, and Darius after several minutes. They were surprised to see Evanna, but she said nothing to them, just hung back and observed us silently. As we progressed, Debbie asked me if I'd been talking with Evanna. I shook my head, unwilling to repeat what I'd been told, still trying to make sense of it and convince myself that Evanna was wrong.

We regrouped with Vancha and Evra a quarter of an hour later. They'd tracked R.V. to a building and were waiting outside for us. "He went in a few minutes ago," Vancha said. "Alice has gone around the back, in case he tries to escape that way." He glanced at Evanna suspiciously. "Are you here to help or hinder, my Lady?"

"Neither, my Prince." She smiled. "I serve merely as a witness."

"Hurm!" he grunted.

I stared up at the building. It was tall and dark, with jagged grey stones and broken windows. There were nine steps leading up to the oversized front door. The steps were cracked and covered with moss. Apart from some more moss and broken windows, it hadn't changed much since my last visit.

"I know this place," I told Vancha, trying to forget about my conversation with Evanna and focus on the business at hand. "It's an old movie theater. This is where the Cirque Du Freak performed when Steve and I were kids. I should have guessed this was where he'd come. It brings everything full circle. Stuff like that is important to a maniac like Steve."

"You shut up about my dad!" Darius growled.

"You think Leonard's inside?" Vancha asked, cuffing Darius around the ear.

"I'm sure of it," I said, wiping streaks of Morgan James's blood from my forehead — there'd been no time to mop myself clean.

"What about Shancus?" Evra hissed. He was trembling with anxiety. "Will he harm my son?"

"Not as long as we hold *his* son captive," I said.

CHAPTER TWENTY

Evra stared at Darius, confused — he knew nothing about the boy — but my old friend trusted me, so he accepted my guarantee.

"How should we play this?" Debbie asked.

"Just march straight in," I said.

"Is that wise?" Vancha asked. "Perhaps we should try to sneak up on them from the back, or via the roof."

"Steve's prepared this for us," I said. "Anything we can think of, you can bet he's already considered. We can't outguess him. We'd be fools to try. I say we go in, face him directly, and pray that the luck of the vampires is with us."

"The luck of the damned," Darius sneered. "You won't beat my father or any vampaneze. We're more than a match for the likes of you."

Vancha studied Darius curiously. He leaned up close, sniffing like a dog. Then he made a small cut on the boy's right arm — Darius didn't even wince — dabbed a finger in the blood that oozed out, and tasted it. He pulled a face. "He's been blooded."

"By my father," Darius said proudly.

"He's a half-vampaneze?" I frowned, glancing at his fingertips — they were unmarked.

"The blood's weak within him," Vancha said. "But

he's one of them. There's just enough blood in his system to ensure he can never regain his humanity."

"Did you volunteer for this, or did Steve force you?" I asked Darius.

"My father wouldn't force me to do anything!" Darius snorted. "Like every vampaneze, he believes in free choice — not like you vampires."

Vancha looked at me questioningly. "Steve's fed him a load of nonsense about us," I explained. "He thinks we're evil, and his father's a noble crusader."

"He is!" Darius shouted. "He'll stop you from taking over the world! He won't let you kill freely! He'll keep the night safe from you vampire scum!"

Vancha cocked an amused eyebrow at me. "If we had time, I'd take great delight in setting this boy straight. But we haven't. Debbie — phone Alice and tell her to come here. We'll go in together — all for one and all that stuff."

While Debbie was on the phone, Vancha pulled me aside and nodded at Evra, who was standing a few yards ahead of us, gazing at the entrance to the theater, fingers twisted into desperate fists. "He's in a bad way," Vancha said.

"Of course," I muttered. "How would you expect him to react?"

"Are you clear on what we must do?" Vancha responded. I stared at him coldly. He grabbed my arms and squeezed tight. "Leonard *must* be killed. You and I are expendable. So are Debbie, Alice, Harkat, Evra — and Shancus."

"I want to save him," I said miserably.

"So do I," Vancha sighed. "And we will, if we can. But the Lord of the Vampaneze comes first. Remember what happens if we fail — the vampires will be destroyed. Would you trade the snake-boy's life for all those of our clan?"

"Of course not," I said, shaking myself free. "But I won't abandon him cheaply. If Steve's prepared to deal, I'll deal. We can fight him some other night."

"And if he won't deal?" Vancha pressed. "If he forces a showdown?"

"Then we'll fight, and we'll kill or we'll die — whatever the cost." I locked gazes with him so he could see I was telling the truth.

Vancha checked his shurikens and drew a few. Then we turned, gathered our allies around us — Debbie dragged Darius along — and advanced up the steps and into the old abandoned movie theater where, for me, all those years ago, the nightmares had begun.

CHAPTER TWENTY-ONE

IT WAS LIKE STEPPING BACK into the past. The building was cooler and damper than before, and fresh graffiti had been scrawled across the walls, but otherwise it was no different. I led the way down the long corridor where Mr. Tall had sneaked up on Steve and me, appearing out of the darkness with that incredible speed and silence that had been his trademark. A left turn at the end. I noted the spot where Mr. Tall had taken and eaten our tickets. Back then, blue curtains had been draped across the entrance to the auditorium. There were no curtains tonight — the only change.

We entered the auditorium, two abreast, Vancha and Alice in front, Debbie and Evra next (Debbie pushing Darius in front of her), then Harkat and me. Evanna drifted along farther back, detached from us by distance and attitude.

It was completely black inside the auditorium. I couldn't see anything. But I could hear deep, muffled breathing, coming from somewhere far ahead of us. "Vancha," I whispered.

"I know," he whispered back.

"Should we move towards it?" I asked.

"No," he replied. "It's too dark. Wait."

A minute passed. Two. Three. I could feel the tension rising, both in myself and those around me. But nobody broke rank or spoke. We stood in the darkness, waiting, leaving the first move to our foes.

Several minutes later, without warning, spotlights were switched on overhead. Everyone gasped and I cried out loud, hunching over, covering my extra-sensitive eyes with my hands. We were defenseless for a few vital seconds. That would have been the ideal time for an attack. I expected vampaneze and vampets to fall upon us, weapons flashing — but nothing happened.

"Are your eyes OK?" Debbie asked, crouching beside me.

"Not really," I groaned, slowly raising my eyelids a fraction, just enough to see out of. Even that was agony.

Holding a hand over my eyes, I squinted ahead and caught my breath. It was good we hadn't advanced.

CHAPTER TWENTY-ONE

The entire floor of the auditorium had been torn out. In its place, spreading from one wall to the other, running from a few yards ahead of us all the way to the foot of the stage, was a giant pit, filled with sharpened stakes.

"Impressive, isn't it?" someone called from the stage. My eyes lifted. It was hard to see, because the lights were being trained on us from above the stage, but I gradually brought the scene into focus. Dozens of tall, thick logs dotted the stage, placed vertically, ideal cover. Sticking out from behind one log near the front was the grinning face of Steve Leopard.

When Vancha saw Steve, he drew a shuriken and threw it at him. But Steve had picked his spot carefully and the throwing star ended up buried in the wood of the log behind which he was standing.

"Bad luck, Sire," Steve laughed. "Care to make it the best throw out of three?"

"Maybe I can get him," Alice muttered, stepping up past Vancha. She raised her pistol and fired, but the bullet penetrated no deeper than the shuriken.

"Is that the preliminaries out of the way, or do you want to take a few more potshots?" Steve called.

"I could possibly leap the pit," Vancha said dubiously, studying the rows of stakes between him and the stage.

"Don't be ridiculous," I grunted. Even vampires had their limits.

"I don't see anybody else," Debbie whispered, casting her eyes around the auditorium. The balcony above us — where I'd spied on Steve and Mr. Crepsley — could have been swarming with vampaneze and vampets, but I didn't think so. I could hear nothing overhead, not even a single heartbeat.

"Where's your army?" Vancha shouted at Steve.

"Around and about," Steve replied sweetly.

"Didn't you bring them with you?" Vancha challenged him.

"Not tonight," Steve said. "I don't need them. The only people sharing the stage with me are my fairy godfather — a.k.a. Gannen Harst — a certain Righteous Vampaneze, and a very scared young snake-boy. What's his name again, R.V.?"

"Shancus," came the reply from behind a log to Steve's left.

"Shancus!" Evra roared. "Are you all right?"

There was no reply. My heart sank. Then R.V. pushed Shancus out from behind the log, and we saw although his hands were tied behind his back and he was gagged, he was still very much alive, and he looked unharmed.

"He's a spirited lad," Steve laughed. "A bit loud

though, hence the gag. Some of the language he uses . . . Shocking! I don't know where kids today pick up such filthy words." Steve paused. "By the way, how's my own beloved flesh and blood doing? I can't see too well from here."

"I'm fine, Dad!" Darius shouted. "But they killed Morgan! The grey one cut off his head with an axe!"

"How grisly." Steve didn't sound the least bit upset. "I told you they were savages, son. No respect for life."

"It was revenge!" Harkat yelled. "He killed Mr. Tall."

There was silence on the stage. Steve seemed at a loss for words. Then, from a log close by Steve, I heard Gannen Harst call out to R.V., "Is this true?"

"Yes," R.V. mumbled. "He shot him."

"How do you know he killed him?" Steve asked. "Tall might have simply been wounded."

"No," Evanna answered, her first word of the encounter. "He is dead. Morgan James murdered him."

"Is that you, Lady Evanna?" Steve asked uncertainly.

"Yes," she said.

"Not up to any mischief, I hope, like siding with the vampires?" He said it flippantly, but his anxiety was evident — he didn't fancy a clash with the Lady of the Wilds.

"I have never taken sides between the vampires and vampaneze, and have no intention of starting now," Evanna said coolly.

"That's OK then," Steve chuckled, confidence returning. "Interesting about Mr. Tall. I always thought he couldn't be killed by ordinary weapons. I'd have gone after him a long time ago if I'd known he could be so easily bumped off."

"Gone after him for what?" I shouted.

"Harboring criminals," Steve giggled.

"You're the only criminal here," I retorted.

Steve sighed theatrically. "See how they slander me, son? They soil this world with their murderous presence, then point the finger of blame elsewhere. That's always been the vampire way."

I started to respond, then decided I'd be wasting my time. "Let's cut the crap," I called instead. "You didn't lead us here for a war of words. Are you coming out from behind that log or not?"

"Not!" Steve cackled. "Do you think I'm insane? You'd cut me down dead!"

"Then why did you bring us here?" I looked around again, nervous. I couldn't believe he hadn't laid a trap, that there weren't dozens of vampaneze or vampets slithering up on us as we talked. Yet I didn't sense a threat. I could see Vancha was confused too.

CHAPTER TWENTY-ONE

"I want to chat, Darren," Steve said. "I'd like to discuss a peace treaty."

I had to laugh at that — it was such a ludicrous notion. "Maybe you want to become my blood-brother," I jeered.

"In a way, I already am," Steve said cryptically. Then his eyes narrowed slyly. "You missed Tommy's funeral while you were recovering."

I cursed fiercely but quietly. "Why kill Tommy?" I snarled. "Why drag him into your warped web of revenge? Did *he* 'betray' you too?"

"No," Steve said. "Tommy was my friend. Even while others were bad-mouthing me, he stuck by me. I had nothing against him. A great goalkeeper too."

"Then why have him killed?" I screamed.

"What are you talking about?" Darius cut in. "*You* killed Tom Jones. Morgan and R.V. tried to stop you, but . . . That's right, isn't it, Dad?" he asked, and I saw the first flickers of doubt stir in the boy's eyes.

"I told you, son," Steve replied, "you can't believe anything a vampire says. Pay no attention to him." Then, to me, he said, "Didn't you wonder how Tommy got his ticket to the Cirque Du Freak?"

"I just assumed . . ." I stopped. "You set him up!"

"Of course," Steve chuckled. "With *your* help. Remember the ticket you gave to Darius? He passed it on. Tommy was opening a sports store, signing autographs. Darius went along and 'swapped' his ticket for a signed soccer ball. We still have it lying around somewhere. Could be a collector's item soon."

"You're sick," I snarled. "Using a child to do your dirty work — disgusting."

"Not really," Steve disagreed. "It just shows how highly I value the young."

Now that I knew Steve had given Tommy the ticket, my mind raced ahead, putting the pieces of his plan together. "You couldn't have known for sure that Tommy would run into me at the show," I said.

"No, but I guessed he would. If he hadn't, I'd have worked out some other way to maneuver you together. I didn't need to, but I liked the idea. Him being here at the same time as us was providence. I'm just slightly miffed that Alan wasn't here too — that would have made for a complete reunion."

"What about my cup ticket? How did you find out about that?"

"I phoned Tommy that morning," Steve said. "He was astonished — first he bumps into his old pal Darren, then he hears from his old buddy Steve. What a coincidence! I faked astonishment too. I asked all about you. Learned that you were coming to the match. He invited me as well, but I said I couldn't make it."

CHAPTER TWENTY-ONE

"Very clever," I complimented him icily.

"Not especially," Steve said with false modesty. "I simply used his innocence to ensnare you. Manipulating the innocent is child's play. I'm surprised you didn't see through it. You need to work on your paranoia, Darren. Suspect everyone, even those beyond suspicion — that's my motto."

Vancha edged up close to me. "If you keep him talking, maybe I can slip out back and attack him from the rear," he whispered.

I nodded my head a fraction and Vancha slid away slowly. "Tommy told me he'd been in contact with you in the past," I said loudly, hoping to mask the sound of Vancha's footsteps. "He said there was something about you that he had to tell me the next time we met, after the match."

"I can guess what that was," Steve purred.

"Care to share it with me?"

"Not yet," he said. Then, sharply, "If you take one more step towards that door, Mr. March, the snake-boy dies." Vancha stopped and shot Steve a look of disgust.

"Leave my son alone!" Evra screamed. He'd been holding himself in check, but Steve's threat proved too much. "If you harm him, I'll kill you! I'll put you through so much agony, you'll pray for death!"

"My!" Steve cooed. "Such vindictiveness! You seem to have the knack of driving all your friends to violence, Darren. Or do you deliberately surround yourself with violent people?"

"Stuff it!" I grunted. Then, tiring of his verbal games, I said, "Are you going to fight or not?"

"I already answered that question," Steve said. "We'll fight soon, have no fear, but this is neither the time nor the place. There's a rear tunnel — newly carved — that we'll leave by shortly. By the time you pick your way through the stakes, we'll be far out of reach."

"Then what are you waiting for?" I snarled. "Get the hell out!"

"Not yet," Steve said, and his voice was hard now. "There's the sacrifice to make first. In the old days, a sacrifice was always made before a large battle, to appease the gods. Now, it's true that the vampaneze don't have any official gods, but to be on the safe side . . ."

"No!" Evra screamed — it was as clear to him as to the rest of us what Steve meant to do.

"Don't!" I shouted.

"Gannen!" Vancha roared. "You can't allow this!"

"I have no say in it, brother," Gannen Harst responded from behind his log. He hadn't shown his face yet. I had the feeling he was ashamed to show it.

"Ready, R.V.?" Steve asked.

"I'm not sure about this, man," R.V. replied uneasily.

"Don't disobey me!" Steve growled. "I made you and I can break you. Now, you bearded, armless freak — are you ready?"

A short pause. Then R.V. answered softly, "Yes."

Vancha cursed and raced forward to force his way through the pit of stakes. Harkat lumbered after him. Alice and Debbie fired on the log protecting Steve, but their bullets couldn't pierce it. I stood, clutching my knife, thinking desperately.

Then a voice behind me called out shakily, "Dad?" Everybody paused. I looked back. Darius was trembling. "Dad?" he called again. "You're not really going to kill him, are you?"

"Be quiet!" Steve snapped. "You don't understand what's happening."

"But . . . he's just a kid . . . like me. You can't —"

"Shut up!" Steve roared. "I'll explain later! Just —"

"No," I interrupted, sliding up behind Darius. "There won't be any 'later.' If you kill Shancus, I'll kill Darius." For the second time that night I felt a dark spirit grow within me, and pressed the blade of my knife to the young boy's throat. Behind me, Evanna made a small cooing noise. I ignored her.

"You're bluffing," Steve jeered. "You couldn't kill a child."

"He could," Debbie answered for me. She stepped away. "Darren was going to kill him earlier. Harkat stopped him. He said we'd need the boy to trade for Shancus. Otherwise Darren would have killed him. Darius — is that the truth?"

"Yes," Darius moaned. He was weeping. Part of it was fear, but an equal part was horror. His father had raised him on lies and false heroics. Only now was he beginning to realize what sort of monster he'd aligned himself with.

I heard Steve mutter something. He peered out from around his log, studying us from the heights of the stage. I made no threatening moves. I didn't need to. My determination was clear.

"Very well," Steve snorted. "Throw away your weapons and we'll swap the two boys."

"You think we'll entrust ourselves to your untender mercies?" Vancha huffed. "Release Shancus and we'll turn your son over."

"Not until you shed your weapons," Steve insisted.

CHAPTER TWENTY-ONE

"And allow you to mow us down?" Vancha challenged him.

There was a short pause. Then Steve threw an arrow-gun away, far across the stage. "Gannen," he said, "am I carrying any other weapons?"

"A sword and two knives," Gannen Harst replied immediately.

"I don't mean those," Steve growled. "Do I have any long-range weapons?"

"No," Gannen said.

"What about you and R.V.?"

"We have none either."

"I know you don't believe a word I say," Steve shouted to Vancha, "but you trust your own brother, don't you? He's a pure vampaneze — he'd kill himself before he'd utter a lie."

"Aye," Vancha muttered unhappily.

"Then throw away your weapons," Steve said. "We won't attack if you don't."

Vancha looked to me for advice. "Do it," I said. "He's tied, just like we are. He won't risk his son's life."

Vancha was dubious, but he slipped off his belts of throwing stars and tossed them aside. Debbie threw her pistols away and so, reluctantly, did Alice. Harkat had only an axe, which he laid down on the floor beside him. I kept my knife to Darius's throat.

Steve stepped out from behind the log. He was grinning. I felt a great temptation to throw my knife at him — I might just have been able to strike him from this distance — but I didn't. As a Vampire Prince, and one of the hunters of the Vampaneze Lord, I should have. But I couldn't risk missing and enraging Steve. He'd kill Shancus if I did.

"Out you come, boys," Steve said. Gannen Harst and R.V. emerged from behind their logs, R.V. shoving the bound Shancus ahead of him. Gannen Harst was typically grim-faced, but R.V. was smiling. At first I thought it was a mocking smile, but then I realized it was a smile of relief — he was delighted he hadn't been called upon to kill the snake-boy. R.V. was a twisted, bitter, crazy man, but I saw then that he wasn't entirely evil — not like Steve.

"I'll take the reptile," Steve said, reaching for Shancus. "You go get the plank and extend it across the pit."

R.V. handed Shancus to Steve and retreated to the rear of the stage. He started dragging a long plank forward. It was awkward for him — he couldn't get a decent grip because of the hooks Mr. Tall had torn off. Gannen went to help him, keeping one eye on us. The pair began feeding the plank across the pit, letting it rest on blunt-tipped stakes, which I could now see had been placed there specifically for this purpose.

Steve watched us like a hawk while R.V. and Gannen were busy with the plank. He was holding Shancus in front of him, stroking the snake-boy's long green hair. I didn't like the way he was looking at us — I felt as though we were being x-rayed — but I said nothing, willing R.V. and Gannen to hurry up with the plank.

Steve's eyes lingered on Evra a long moment — he was smiling hopefully, hands half-reaching out to his son — then settled on me. He stopped stroking Shancus's hair and gently placed a hand on either side of his head. "Remember the games we played when we were children?" he asked craftily.

"What games?" I frowned. I had a terrible feeling — a sense of total doom — but I could do nothing but follow his lead.

"'Dare' games," Steve said, and something in his voice made R.V. and Gannen pause and look around. Steve's face was expressionless, but his eyes were alive with insane glee. "One of us would say, 'I dare you to do this,' and stick his hand in a fire or jab a pin in his leg. The other would have to copy him. Remember?"

"No!" I moaned. I knew what was coming. I knew I couldn't stop it. I knew I'd been a fool and made a fool's mistake — I'd assumed Steve was even the slightest bit human.

"I dare you to do this, Darren," Steve whispered dreadfully. Before I could reply — before anything else could happen — he seized Shancus's head tightly and twisted it sharply to the left, then the right. Shancus's neck snapped. Steve dropped him. Shancus fell to the floor. Steve had killed him.

CHAPTER TWENTY-TWO

STEVE'S ACT OF PURE, pointless evil caught everyone by gut-wrenching surprise. For a long moment we just stared at him and the lifeless body by his feet. Even Steve looked stunned, as though he'd acted without thinking it through.

Then Evra went wild. "*Bastard!*" he screamed, hurling himself at the pit of stakes. If Harkat hadn't reacted and knocked him aside, Evra would have impaled himself on the stakes and died like his son.

"I can't believe . . ." Alice muttered, face whiter than usual. Then her features hardened and she ran for the pistol she'd discarded.

Debbie sank to her knees, weeping, unable to deal with such wickedness. As hardened as she'd become, nothing in her life had prepared her for this.

Harkat was struggling with Evra, pinning him down, protecting him from his rage. Evra was screaming hysterically and pounding Harkat's broad grey face with his scaly fists, but Harkat held firm.

Vancha was at the pit of stakes, lurching through them, clambering over the sharpened tips, driving towards the stage like a man possessed.

R.V. and Gannen Harst were staring at Steve, jaws slack.

Evanna was looking on silently. If the murder had shocked her, she was masking it incredibly well.

Darius was stiff with terror, holding his breath, eyes wide.

I was still behind Darius, my knife at his throat. I was the calmest of everyone there (except Evanna). Not because I was in any way unaffected by what had happened, but because I knew what I must do in retaliation. The fierce, hard, hating part within me had flared to life and taken over completely. I saw the world through different eyes. It was a dreadful, wicked place, where only the dreadful and wicked could prosper. To defeat an evil monster like Steve, I had to sink to his depths myself. Mr. Crepsley had warned me not to, but he was wrong. What did it matter if I followed Steve down the road of total evil? Stopping him —

getting revenge for all the people he'd killed — was the only thing I cared about now.

While I was thinking all this through, Gannen snapped to his senses and saw that Vancha was closing in on them. He hurried to his Lord, grabbed Steve by the right arm, and spun him towards the exit, cursing foully. R.V. rose shakily and stumbled after them. He stopped, vomited, then reeled ahead.

Alice found her pistol, brought it up, and fired. But there were too many logs between her and the vampaneze. She didn't even get close to them.

Steve stopped by the tunnel entrance at the rear of the stage. Gannen tried to push him down it, but he shook his protector's hands away and turned to glare triumphantly — daringly — at me.

"Go on!" Steve screamed. "Show me you can do it! I dare you! I double dare you!"

In that moment, as if our minds were somehow joined, I understood Steve entirely. Part of him was appalled by his brutality. He was hanging dangerously on the edge of outright madness. As the monster within me had grown this night, so had the human within Steve. He needed me to match his evil deeds. If I killed Darius, Steve could justify his cruelty and continue. But if I didn't respond to his evil with an equally evil act of my own, it would drive home the truth about how far he'd fallen. He might even snap beneath the weight of full realization and go mad. I had the power to destroy him — with mercy.

But I couldn't find mercy within myself. The fires of fury in my heart and head demanded I kill Darius. Right or wrong, I had to avenge Shancus's death. An eye for an eye, a tooth for a tooth, a life for a life. Out of the corner of one eye I caught sight of Evanna. Her gaze was locked on me. There was no pity in her expression, merely the weariness of one who has seen all the evils of the world and must watch them repeat themselves over and over again.

"Dare accepted," I said, abandoning myself to my dark destiny, knowing in that moment that I was betraying all my moral beliefs. This was the start of the path to damnation. If I defeated Steve, I *would* become the Lord of the Shadows, and in the long, blood-red decades and centuries ahead, I'd be able to point back to this night and say, "That was where the monster was born."

I began to draw my knife across Darius's throat. This time Debbie didn't try to stop me — she sensed my damnation, and was powerless to save me. But then I paused. The throat was too impersonal a target. I wanted Steve to really *feel* this.

CHAPTER TWENTY-TWO

Lowering the knife, I cut away Darius's shirt, revealing his bare, pale chest. I positioned the tip of the knife over his heart and gazed at Steve, no longer blinking against the searing lights, my eyes dark, my lips tight over my teeth.

Steve's expression steadied. The beast within him had seen its mirror image in me, and was satisfied. He drew back from the madness, becoming his cold, crafty, calculating self again. He smiled.

I drew my arm back to its full extent, so I could strike swiftly with the knife. I meant to stab Darius with all my strength and kill him quickly. I might be a monster, but I wasn't an entirely heartless one. At least, not yet.

But Steve called out before I pierced his son's heart. "Be careful, Darren! You don't know who you're killing!"

I shouldn't have hesitated. I knew, if I did, that he'd derail me with some other twisted trick. Listening to demons was dangerous. Better to act in haste and shut your ears to them.

But I couldn't help myself. There was something darkly inviting about his tone. It was like when someone was about to tell a gruesome but hilarious joke. I could feel the awfulness of it, but also the humor. I had to hear him out.

"Darius," Steve chuckled, "tell Darren your mother's name." Darius gaped at his father, unable to respond. "Darius!" Steve roared. "He's about to drive a knife through your heart! Tell him your mother's name — now!"

"Ah-ah-ah-Annie," Darius wheezed, and I froze.

"And her surname?" Steve asked softly, relishing the moment.

"Shan," Darius whispered uncomprehendingly. "Annie Shan. What about it?"

"You see, Darren," Steve purred, winking at me before vanishing down the tunnel to freedom, "if you kill Darius, you won't just be slaughtering my son — you'll be murdering *your nephew*!"

TO BE CONCLUDED IN SONS OF DESTINY, THE STUNNING FINALE TO THE CIRQUE DU FREAK SERIES.

Book 1

Darren Shan is just an ordinary schoolboy—until he gets an invitation to visit the Cirque Du Freak. Soon, Darren and his friend Steve are caught in a deadly trap. Darren must make a bargain with the one person who can save Steve. But that person is not human and deals only in blood. . . .

Book 2

CIRQUE DU FREAK The Vampire's Assistant

THE SAGA OF DARREN SHAN

As a vampire's assistant, Darren struggles to resist the one temptation that sickens him—the one thing that can keep him alive. But destiny is calling—the wolf-man is waiting.

Book 3

CIRQUE DU FREAK Tunnels of Blood

THE SAGA OF DARREN SHAN

When corpses are discovered—drained of blood—Darren and Evra are compelled to hunt down whatever foul creature is committing such acts. Beneath the streets, evil stalks. Can they escape, or are they doomed to perish in the tunnels of blood?

Darren Shan and Mr. Crepsley embark on a dangerous trek to the very heart of the vampire world. Will a meeting with the Vampire Princes restore Darren's human side, or push him further towards the darkness?

Darren Shan must pass five fearsome Trials to prove himself to the vampire clan—or face the stakes in the Hall of Death. But Vampire Mountain holds hidden threats. In this nightmarish world of bloodshed and betrayal, death may be a blessing.

Can Darren, the vampire's assistant, reverse the odds and outwit a Vampire Prince, or is this the end of thousands of years of vampire rule?

As part of an elite force, Darren searches the world for the Vampaneze Lord. But the road ahead is long and dangerous—and lined with the bodies of the damned.

Book 8

Allies of the Night

Darren Shan, Vampire Prince and vampaneze killer, faces his worst nightmare yet—school! But homework is the least of Darren's problems. Bodies are piling up. Time is running out.

Book 9

Killers of the Dawn

Pursued by the vampaneze, the police, and an angry mob, Darren Shan the Vampire Prince is public enemy number one! With their enemies clamoring for blood, the vampires prepare for a deadly battle. Is this the end for Darren and his allies?

Darren and Harkat face monstrous obstacles on their desperate quest to the Lake of Souls. Will they survive the savage journey? And what awaits them in the murky waters of the dead? Be careful what you fish for. . . .

The Demonata exist in a multi-world universe of their own.
Evil, murderous creatures who revel in torment and slaughter.
They try to cross over into our world all the time.

Don't miss Darren Shan's
chilling DEMONATA series.

And watch out for *Slawter* (Book 3),
coming November 2006.